On Behalf Of Earthlings

Author:

Rhoan Flowers

Artists:

Jahvon Flowers

Rhovon Flowers

On Behalf Of Earthlings
Navan, Ontario
Canada

Published by: Rhoan Flowers Books

Cover Design: Clyde Williams

Released: December 2023

Genre: Young Adult's Book

ISBN: 978-1-989995-13-6 {H.C}

ISBN: 978-1-989995-14-3 {E.B}

Library & Archives of Canada

395 Wellington Street

Ottawa, Ontario

K1A-0N4

On Behalf of Earthlings

Planet Zurue was home to many different and unique creatures, however, its most dominating and intellectual being was the Zuruevians. The Zuruevians were a species with similar body composition to humans; except they had thin black feathers covering their entire bodies to retain heat. Their heads were shaped like cubes, had broad rectangular eyes, a pair of tiny holes for breathing, and split lips at either ends of their mouth. The Zuruevians had three wide fingers on both hands and three wide toes, all of which had a wide hardened claw made from Keratin. The most distinctive feature of the Zuruevian was their purple complexion, beneath their shield of thin black feathers. As a species they were considered the tallest throughout the Universe, with an average height of 7ft for the females and 9ft for males.

With the life of their planet coming to an end, ten finalists from whom the judges were to select two cadets to join the most illustrious exploration team in history, gathered inside the mission's headquarters. All the cadets stood at attention in a straight line, while they awaited their commanding officers. Each cadet had performed admirably during the competition exercises, however, there were only two other astronauts required. There were twenty-eight pilots already selected, who were considered the very best at the training academy. Although the winners would be celebrated for their heroism, their explorations were widely considered the bitter-sweet moment in all their careers. The candidates knew there was no returning from their voyages, additionally they could perish during the mission, nevertheless they all boldly volunteered.

The mood inside the hall was intense, as the twenty-eight preselected pilots stood closest to the podium and waited. The highest ranked junior pilot inside the hall was Junior Commandant Zonk, who was only sixteen. All the candidates were children, some as young as ten-years-old, but none beyond the age of sixteen. When the door attendant signaled their commanders were approaching, Junior Commandant Zonk yelled orders for every candidate to salute. Three of the base commanding officers entered the hall and stepped onto the podium. With his two associates standing behind him, Chief Commander Ibik stepped forward and addressed the candidates.

"Relax," Chief Commander Ibik instructed in Zuruevian language at which the officers and cadets complied! "I will make this short and precise! Cadet Azka, Congratulations! Cadet Ruku, Congratulations! Welcome to the team! I am sure you will make this academy and your family all proud," Chief Commander Ibik stated before he and his commanders left the podium and exited the hall!

The trainees all quickly saluted their commanders as they exited the mission headquarters. As soon as the commanders went through the entrance and the doors reclosed, the other cadets began cheering and celebrating the winners. The twenty-eight preselected astronauts were unimpressed with the two cadets selected and thereafter walked out without offering any acknowledgements. Despite the lack of recognition from the other selected pilots, the winners jumped around and celebrated the achievements with their fellow cadets. There was a large reward being offered to the explorer who was successful on the mission, so everyone had huge incentives to win.

Cadet Azka and Cadet Ruku were great friends since childhood and grew up in the same neighbourhood. Contrary to the twenty-eight elite students, Azka and Ruku were from lower ranked families who received subsidies to attend the flight academy. Understanding from where they came and the sacrifices made to get them there, both cadets performed at their highest levels to edge out the other competitors. The members of the Elite Flying Squad thought none of the cadets who received grants to attend their institution should be allowed to compete, but that decision was not theirs to make. Immediately after the celebrations with their peers, both cadets contacted their loved ones to provide them with the news. The tasks before them made their conversations with their families rather emotional, considering they might not survive the journey.

It had been nearly half a century since the Tectonic Plates deep underground the Planet of Zurue became unstable and ruptured. Since then, the residents began experiencing larger than normal earthquakes, on a more consistent basis. The entire surface of Zurue eventually became uninhabitable; however, the locals had reconstructed and elevated their cities on thick metallic plates. To anchor their cities the residents built huge metal pillars, which were extended far into the ground. With more devastating tremors unleashed throughout the decades, the structural stability around several pillars eventually weakened. Whenever infrastructure damages occurred due to soil depletion around the pillars, entire neighbourhoods were either lost or badly destroyed, as such the residents began looking to the stars for a new life.

One of the locals' first response to the rupture, was to design and engineer single-manned exploration spacecrafts, to explore and locate a new habitable planet. While the exploration vessels were being designed, a second team of engineers developed the main brain for each spaceship. To create a device that would also protect the operators of the vessels without them being inside the cockpit, the inventors designed a small orb that could also be inserted into their spacesuits. The creators of the orb thought of numerous life-threatening situations and designed it to provide multiple aid to its user. Within fifteen years of realizing their planet was doomed, the locals invented and constructed a fleet of thirty exploration vessels.

The residents of Zurue had no scientific evidence there was another habitable planet out in the Universe, nevertheless they had no choice but to search for a new home. To find a new habitable planet the leaders requested volunteers at specific ages to pilot the exploration spacecrafts. Twenty-eight of the thirty young volunteers were members of an elite flying squad, while the other two pilots only volunteered to save their families and species. The candidates were all put through the most rigorous and mentally challenging training, to prepare them for their long and solitary exploration. Even though the volunteers were all assigned to the same division, the twenty-eight elite flyers spent much of their time together or in private consultations with Chief Commander Ibik.

Chief Commander Ibik, Second Commander Xong, and Third Commander Kzaw stood before Emperor Zura and the members of their National Council, providing an update on the status of their program. The idea of sending children into space on expeditions to locate a new planet, had become a reality. Instilling such a responsibility on teenagers was debated across the empire, but the decision was eventually agreed upon, because younger aged pilots provided more time for them to locate a planet. Although the decision had been finalized, some of the council members were still opposed to the idea and wanted their older pilots to man the mission.

"Members of council, all of our pilots have successfully passed their flight training and have begun getting acclimated to the new exploration crafts," Second Commander Xong explained!

"Will they be prepared to leave on schedule," Council Member 11 asked?

"They will, Council Member 11," Second Commander Xong answered!

"Chief Commander Ibik, according to the psychological evaluation of your candidates, some examiners fear that more than half your students might suffer from mental collapse due to the overall stress of this mission! Why do you not call this kidding around a failure, so we can use our more talented and qualified pilots," Council Member 8 asked?

"Council Member 8, all of the pilots are confident they will complete their mission," Chief Commander Ibik responded!

"Emperor Zura, we cannot put our future in the care of mentally weak children! None of these children should be allowed to negotiate on our behalf! Nor should any of them be allowed the use of Spec of Light," Council Member 8 declared!

Emperor Zura signalled everyone to cease talking, then considered the different opinions he heard from his advisers. Following a short delay, the emperor spoke and gave his judgement. "Whosoever discovers our new planet, must only ensure that the surface is habitable! Once accomplished, they must return to the boundaries of space, and remain there until our convoy arrives! Chief Commander Ibik, you will ensure that the Spec of Light has been deactivated on all expedition vessels," Emperor Zura ordered then rose from his throne and exited!

Cadet Ruku and Cadet Azka were training inside the flying facility's simulation chambers. Both young pilots were practicing evasive maneuvers inside the replicative machines, which tested their abilities to control their aircrafts during pivotal and dangerous incidents. Although they practiced in separate simulation chambers, the close friends were able to speak to each other over their microphones during the process.

"I can not wait until we get to join their elite club," Cadet Ruku stated!

"Why do you want to join them? Can you not tell they don't like us? Plus, there is something weird about them," Cadet Azka responded!

"That is why we must join the club. To get to know them," Cadet Ruku joked!

Inside a separate section of the facility, the twenty-eight preselected elite pilots were seated on the floor with their legs crossed. The room was dark with no one else present to monitor the students. All the pilots were focused on a tiny white hole in the wall ahead of them, through which they saw a hypnotizing figure. The image they saw was of their ruler, who wore a cloak and hid his face among the shadows during his address. There were also subtle mesmerizing images of their species toiling under dictatorship within the video, that captivated the students while they watched.

"You will plunder and annihilate all species that already exist on your new planet! Unless you are prepared to wipe out all alien creatures, you might become a servant of those creatures! Zuruevians serve no one…"

Chief Commander Ibik, Second Commander Xong, and Third Commander Kzaw monitored the pilots from a secret room. While they closely monitored the young pilots, a notification alert sounded to which Chief Commander Ibik responded. Once the three main administrators saw who the contact was, they immediately bowed their heads in rendering respect.

"Lord Ozar," Chief Commander Ibik stated!

"I take it our special training has been successful," Lord Ozar lamented!

"Yes, Lord Ozar," Chief Commander Ibik responded!

"Excellent," Lord Ozar said before the link disconnected!

As the final days before the pilots' departure ticked away, Azka and Ruku grew increasingly afraid, while their elite comrades pretended as though they were unfazed by the pressures of the mission. Even though they shared the same training facility for years, none of the elite pilots acknowledged their cohorts under any circumstance. All the pilots were awarded the opportunity to spend the last day before their historic flights, with a limited number of their family members. Rather than inviting their loved ones to the base, the twenty-eight elite pilots contacted them via video chat, then spent the remainder of the day locked inside their meditation chamber. Contrary to their team members, the eleven-year-olds could not wait to see their family members, whom they had not seen since they enlisted.

The families all met inside the visitor's hall, where they decided to join tables to support each other. There were only immediate family members allowed during the visit, to provide every pilot with enough space for their relatives. Ruku and Azka thought their comrades and family members would be present, therefore they were surprised when no one else attended. The elite pilots' absence made it easier for the newest trainees to openly express their emotions, thereby they were abled to received positive feedbacks in return.

Even though they were tasked with the most important mission throughout their history, once Ruku saw his parents Uvak and Zurro he ran directly into their arms. Xuru his brother was already well beyond the age required for volunteering; therefore, he was assigned to work on the construction of their spaceships. Azka's mother and father attended with his two younger sisters Yamak and Koura. As soon as Azka walked into his family's arms he began crying. The family embraced for a while, before they all took a seat around the table. There was already refreshments and fruits available on the table, so Azka's mother Kazar fixed everyone beverages. Zaku his father knew exactly what plagued his son, so before Azka uttered a word he spoke.

"I know that, what everyone asks of you both is difficult, but we, your family needs you to save us! Azka, Ruku, unless you find our new planet, we are all doomed," began Zaku!

"Ruku, Azka, we are all going to miss you! But we know you can do this, for…" Uvak began!

Without any warning the room began shaking as they experienced an earthquake. Both fathers rushed their family members underneath the tables to avoid any injuries. Despite the scare, being abled to spend time with their families at that junction, helped to reassure why and for whom they became explorers.

The pilots' living quarters were divided between two floors, with rooms along both sides of the corridor. There was a pane of glass built into each door, to allow security to look in on each pilot. Neither Ruku nor Azka could sleep a wink that night, as anticipation made them eager to see the morning's daylight. Regardless of the elite pilots' discriminatory ways, Azka felt the urge to wish Junior Commandant Zonk and some of their cohorts a safe voyage. It was late in the night and everyone's suite he passed had an occupant who was sound asleep, so Azka went to check if Zonk was awake. As he approached their junior commander's living quarters, he overheard a male's voice inside the room, so Azka hid by the door and listened.

"… this to summon the rest of your team! Once we have located our new planet and you are made grand champion, I shall give you the signal, and you will strike him down! With his perishing, I will be made ruler, and you as grand champion, will become my successor," declared the male's voice!

"I will do as you command my Lord," Junior Commandant Zonk stated!

Once Azka overheard their discussion and realized that the male was taking his leave, he quickly entered another elite pilot's room and hid behind the door. Azka did not wish to get caught and remained quiet while the male visitor went by the suite. While hiding inside the living quarters, Azka was startled when the occupant sat up in bed with his eyes closed, then bowed his head as the male walked by. When the elite student went back to sleep, Azka breathed a sigh of relief knowing he would have gotten in serious trouble if caught. After he felt confident enough to leave, the young pilot began sneaking his way from the suite. Zonk was hiding the device inside his flight suit when he overheard a sound, so he looked out the door and caught a glimpse of Azka turning the corner.

Following the earthquake all the exploration vessels had to get inspected before the missions were approved. There were no grand celebrations involving fireworks or street parades to celebrate the departing explorers, yet their loved ones and crouds of Zuruevians gathered at observation stations to watch the vessels launch into space. Each spacecraft was constructed inside a tube, which propelled them to electrifying speeds at departure. Ruku and Azka were the last two exploration pilots ascended into space, all of whom carried the hopes and prayers of an entire civilization.

Five years had passed since they deployed the fleet of explorers without a response, however, to save the rest of their population they built seven humongous spaceships. Each space vessel was uniquely customized to transport cargo, livestock, and personnel. It was impossible for them to reverse their planet's misfortune, therefore their only means of survival was to relocate elsewhere. Even though the impending disaster seemed assured, there were activists who disagreed with abandoning the planet, and argued they should stay. Contrary to all the previous chatter, when the time came for them to leave, everyone packed their belongings and boarded a spaceship. With their entire surviving population and the necessities to survive for several years aboard their escape vessels, the fleet of spaceships prepared for departure. Many of those aboard the vessels cried as they prepared to leave the only home they had ever known. Every resident of Zurue felt heartbroken and unsure of their future, not knowing if there was another world out there for them to inhabit.

Space Transporter I: "Blast-off in 5…4…3…2…1! Ignition," commented the first captain!

Space Transporter II: "Blast-off in 5…4…3…2…1! Ignition," commented the second commander!

Space Transporter III: "Blast-off in 5…4…3…2…1! Ignition," commented the third captain!

Space Transporter IV: "Blast-off in 5…4…3…2…1! Ignition," commented the fourth commander!

Space Transporter V: "Blast-off in 5…4…3…2…1! Ignition," commented the fifth captain!

Space Transporter VI: "Blast-off in 5…4…3…2…1! Ignition," commented the sixth commander!

Space Transporter VII: "Blast-off in 5…4…3…2…1! Ignition," commented the seventh captain!

All seven spaceships ascended into space and acquired a safe distance from Planet Zurue, which was projected to explode months after their departure. The commanders aboard each vessel, did not wish for their spacecrafts to get damaged or destroyed by flying debris from their planet, therefore they quickly expanded the distance between Zurue and their fleet. Each of the seven spaceships had less than a million residents aboard, along with vegetation, minerals, and many of their animal species. While cruising along deep in outer space five weeks later, their home Planet Zurue exploded and lit up the darkness for miles away. The destruction of their home planet was the final confirmation, that unless their scouts discovered a new planet on which to reside, they would die floating around in outer space.

Planet Earth

Twin brothers Draymond and Raymond Thornton were recently graduated high school students, who aspired to become astronauts or space engineers. The eighteen-year-olds lived with their parents several miles east of Okanagan, BC, which had been slowly recovering from a wildfire incident, that scorched hundreds of acres, homes, and businesses across the province. The brothers' father Edmond Thornton was a former astronaut who had to resign from the program after he suffered a spine injury during a training exercise. Their father's injury left him paralyzed in a wheelchair, nevertheless the accident did not dampen his spirit or his love for aerodynamics and space aviation. Dee Thornton, who generally managed the household was scheduled to visit her parents in Trinidad & Tobago for several weeks, however she was terrified about leaving her boys unattended. The family's residence was twenty miles away from the closest fire station; therefore, Mrs. Thornton had reasonable concerns about her mad scientists and their experiments.

The Thornton males had been working on an invention for nearly eight years, which they hoped would revolutionize how fast humans travelled across the globe. When Edmond inherited his father's 1963 Classic, he had no idea what to do with the car until his spinal injury accident. Once he became unable to drive and Dee confiscated his muscle car, Edmond thought of a concept and found inspiration in doing something he truly enjoyed. Watching her husband regained his passion initially enlightened Dee, who encouraged him to pursue whatever he chose to do after his injury. But when a minor explosion piqued her curiosity and she snuck into the garage to snoop, her decision entirely changed. The twins and their father had transformed the 1963 Classic, into a hovering aircraft that looked more like a flight risk. There were thrusters built along both sides of the car to keep it stable and a pair of retractable booster exhaust pipes installed to the rear. The tires were also retractable and functioned perfectly whenever the car drove along roadways.

"I want all this shut down now," warned Dee with her Trinidadian accent!

"Who made mom get in," Raymond stated?

"Yeah, which one of you dummies left the door open," Edmond quarrelled?

"You did Dad, you came in last" Draymond responded!

"Oh, my bad," Edmond said!

"Don't you worry bout how I get in here! What do you think y'all doing? I said, shut that down," Dee yelled!

"Damn! Mom sounds mad," Draymond declared as he dropped the wrench!

"You think Sherlock! So, this is why y'all keep the doors locked all this time? What I want to know is? Which one of you think you go get inside that damn thing and drive it," Dee quarrelled?

"Mom, even dad could handle..." Raymond began.

"Did I ask you a question? Shut up when I'm talking! I told you to shut that car off! I'll be damned if I going to attend any of you funeral," Dee continued!

"Do as your moms said son, and shut it off," Edmond instructed Draymond.

"But Dad what about all that soar through the clouds stuff you were talking about," Draymond exclaimed?

"The only soaring you need do, is soar inside that car, turn it off, and give me the key," Dee instructed!

"Come on Dad say something! You can't just let her win with this one," Raymond declared!

"Yeah Dad, how are we going to become space technicians if we don't do space stuff," Draymond said?

"Yes, I is listening! You think I will ever forget the day I get that phone call saying you was in accident; and how close we come to losing you," Dee exclaimed with tears in her eyes!?

"Son your mother is right! We should have thought of how she would feel about this," Edmond stated.

Draymond climbed into the vehicle and paused looking around at what could have been. The disappointed youth then turned off the engine and removed the key from the ignition. Dee knew her sons were pranksters and therefore walked to an area where she could watch Draymond perform the task. As soon as the young man stepped from the vehicle, his mother was standing right there with her outstretched hand. Although her males were disappointed, Dee felt assured with the car key in hand that they were grounded. Regardless of their mother's personal stance on the issue, Raymond and Draymond knew that taking chances was the livelihood of space explorers, therefore they felt betrayed that Edmond failed to argue their case.

Rather than prolonging an argument he would not win, Edmond waited until Dee had exited the garage, then slowly withdrew a spare car key, and jiggled it around. Both Draymond and Raymond started giggling with their father, who made Dee assumed as though she had won their dispute. For the next two weeks however the garage was closed, while the technicians did other boring chores around the yard. The Thornton males knew that Dee had a prescheduled flight to Trinidad & Tobago, therefore they patiently waited until the date of her flight. Before leaving for the airport, Dee made sure that she locked the car key inside her luggage, where none of her males could get to it. Edmond and the boys pretended as though they were deeply saddened to see Dee leave, but as soon as the cab driver pulled away from the house, they were racing to the garage.

All the systems incorporated into the 63 Classic were functional, but the inventors had not yet taken it for its debut test drive. The car's interior was transformed, after Edmond removed all the original components and welded in a pair of space shuttle seats. The entire vehicle was recoated with the same carbon phenolic composite used to protect shuttle noses, then reinforced with steel to withstand G-force pressures. Edmond purchased a jet concept engine on the Black Market, then upgraded it to perform faster and more efficient.

The designated drivers were the twins, who changed into their jet suits, which were designed to keep their blood flowing during mac speeds. Once the brothers dressed, with their helmets on and breathing masks connected, Edmond buckled them tightly into their seats. The family lived in a rural area; therefore, they had no concerns about nosy neighbours reporting their activities. Draymond drove from the garage and stopped in the yard, where Raymond began transforming the car into a flying vessel. When the thrusters along the sides of the vehicle lifted it off the ground, the co-pilot retracted the wheels and closed the wheel-well. Edmond could communicate with both his sons through their headsets; hence, with all the systems positive, he gave them the green light to launch.

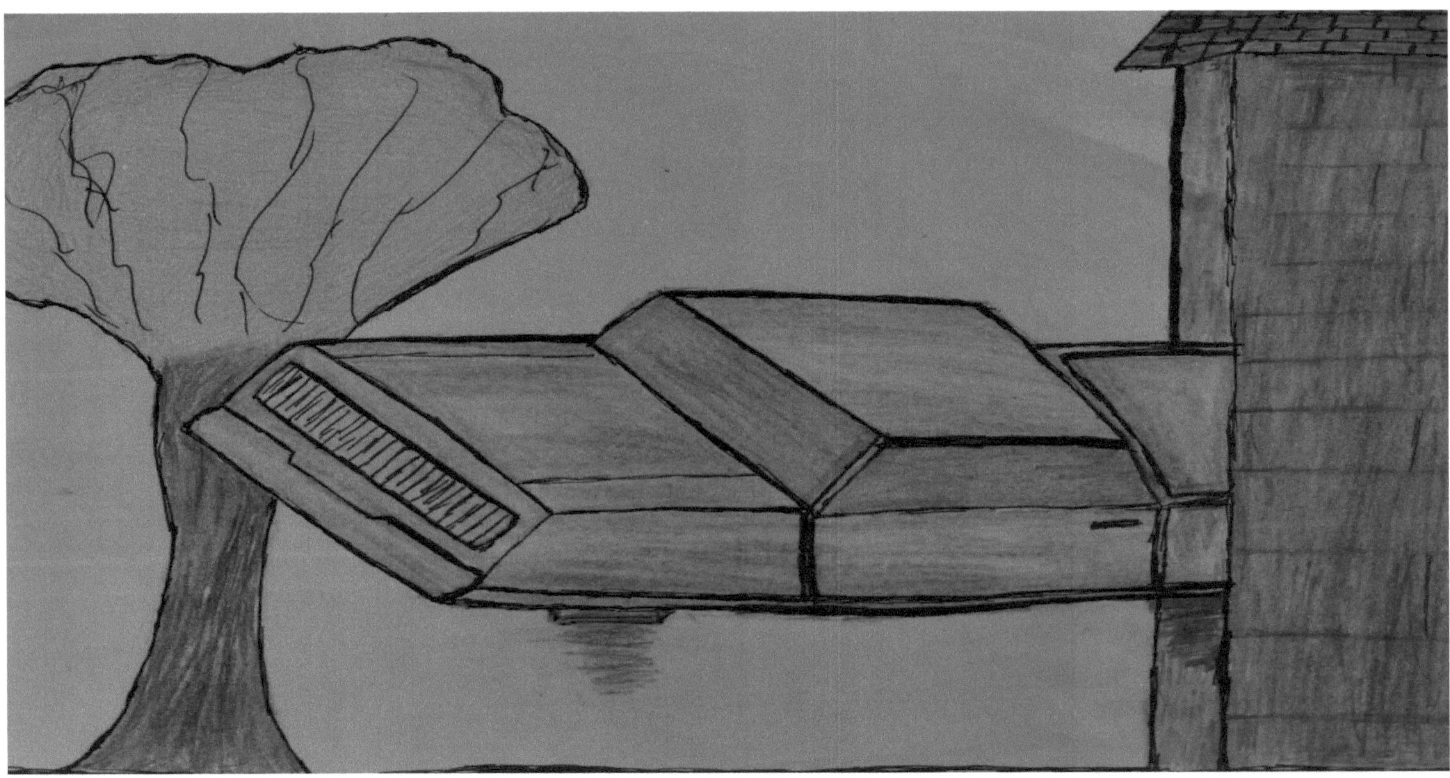

The alien colony had planned to vacate Zurue within five years of their scouts' departure, fearing the projected date of their planet's destruction might come sooner. With more than two trillion galaxies throughout the universe, the thirty explorers charted their individual maps as they voyaged from planet to planet. Once an alien vessel documented a galaxy, that information got sent to all the other spacecrafts. It had been a disappointing search for all the scouts after ten years, wherein none of them discovered a habitable planet. The sensors on their spaceships equipped them to identify the types of landmasses they surpassed; therefore, each planet-like orb was automatically scanned to acquire a correct reading of its surface type and the atmospheric gases.

Traveling between galaxies and planets was an aging and time-consuming process, therefore the explorers would program their controls to auto-pilot and slept. As the years went by, each explorer grew taller and taller while they transformed into adults. With so much time spent in solitude, the main concern for explorers was their mental stability. Throughout their training for the mission, the astronauts underwent vigorous mental exercises to ensure they remained physically capable to perform their duties. Regardless of their preparations, the trainers knew it would be a massive challenge for their explorers to maintain their sanity during the long solitary voyages. Each explorer was encouraged to bring along items that would remind them of who they were and the importance of their mission.

While Azka's exploration vessel sped towards the Milky Way Galaxy, he tussled about in his seat experiencing nightmares. The last explorer to depart from Planet Zurue, was envisioning the locals on his planet, undergoing massive difficulties. Azka dreamt of his loved ones rushing to get aboard one of the escape vessels, during a widespread panic by all the citizens. A massive earthquake had opened a huge crevice in the surface below, which dislodged several columns, ruptured explosions, and wiped out a large section of the city. There were spaceships departing, although crowds of residents were rushing to get aboard other waiting ships. As his loved ones joined a line to board a spaceship, an explosion erupted close to their location, which sent sharp metallic objects crashing into the frame of their vessel. Everyone began screaming and panicking once they realized their escape ship had gotten damaged, therefore Azka's overall vision of the travesty transformed to outer space. The exploration pilot began envisioning his home planet from the final image he captured during his departure, hence Azka frightfully flinched when the planet exploded into large pieces. The nightmare felt so intense that as Azka watched a large fraction of Planet Zurue hurling towards his spacecraft, his heartrate gradually increased faster and faster. The warning sirens inside his cockpit began sounding simultaneously and startled the explorer, who franticly awoke from his nightmare.

When the planetary sensor on Azka's vessel detected their arrival, the ship released a mist of gas through the vents; before the warning alert sounded. Immediately after he inhaled the gas, Azka became alert as if he had been manually flying the spaceship. The sun was extremely hot and bright to the north-east of his exploration vessel, so Azka first lowered the protective blocker inside his ship. Zuruevians were not accustomed to the heat and originated from a planet with an average temperature of -73 Degrees Celsius. One-third of their planet was covered with volcanic activities and heated tar pits, which helped to balance the frigid temperature. After visiting hundreds of galaxies over the years, Azka felt encouraged by what he saw of the Milky Way Galaxy and thought there might be a planet capable to sustain life.

To develop a list of the worthwhile planets he should inspect, Azka used his vessel's main operator to draft a diagram of the galaxy. With the diagram charted, he began running an analysis to determine which were stars and gas planets versus landmass surfaces. When the analysis was complete the main operator determined that there were at lease five hundred million planets of interest. Azka had no time to determine where he should begin, so he programed his main operator to pilot the ship to the closest planet on the list. Even though the analysis had concluded that there were potential planets of interest, many of them were dead planets with no oxygen, vegetation, water, or signs of life.

After another eleven months of searching through the Milky Way Galaxy, Azka began focusing on the third planet from the sun. Zuruevians were accustomed to cold weather, so Azka wanted to find a planet much further away from the Sun's furnace. The heat of the Sun was so devastating even at 93 million miles away to Planet Earth, that the alien wondered if the planet was too warm for his species. The planetary sensors on his vessel began providing irregular readings, compared to all the other planets he had visited. An analysis of the atmosphere revealed that there were greenhouse gases such as Carbon Dioxide (CO_2), Methane (CH_4), Nitrous Oxide (N_2O) Perfluorocarbons (PFCs), Nitrogen Trifluoride (NF_3), Sulphur Hexafluoride (SF_6), and Hydrofluorocarbons (HFCs). Contrary to the amount of greenhouse gases, the planet had all the amenities and more than he was searching for. Before activating the home-in device, the astronauts were advised to inspect the planet first, to ensure the analysis he received was correct. With the number of satellites and space junk in orbit around Planet Earth, Azka felt assured the surface was inhabited, however, what type of species were they?

"**W**hoo-hoo! Yow Dad, this is so much fun! We're going like Mac-3 up here," Draymond yelled!

"Dad this like next level awesome! No wonder you loved being an astronaut," Raymond shouted!

"I know it's an adrenaline rush; but be serious boys! This is serious business at the speed you guys are going," Edmond stated!

"Yeah, you're right! Of course, Dad," Draymond answered!

"All the sensors look great. Draymond, you can bump her up to Mac-4 and let's see how she performs," Edmond exclaimed.

"Sure Dad, increasing speed," Draymond declared.

"I can't wait until it's my turn to drive next test! Oh man we're going fast," Raymond remarked!

"Raymond, I want you to activate the auto pilot, and let's see how well the AI-system controls that car," Edmond stated.

"Activating auto pilot right now Dad," Raymond exclaimed!

The silver colored 1963 Classic, wisped across the top of tall trees, buildings, and residences with such speed, that nobody could capture a snapshot of it. The vehicle's underneath was completely covered with a sheet of metal; therefore, it was difficult to identify the type of transport it was from certain angles. All the upgraded glasses throughout the vehicle were darkly tinted, which made it difficult to see inside.

"This is your AI controller Max! I will be taking control of the vehicle in three, two, one," the AI voice stated through the speakers.

"Dad, that's crazy! You added an actual voice to the AI-system," Draymond exclaimed!

"Hello Draymond and Raymond! Do either of you have a request for me," Max the AI voice asked?

"Max, I want you to maintain your speed! You can do some twirls or whatever maneuvers you have in your database, but maintain this speed for five minutes, then increase to Mac-8," Edmond instructed!

"Command received, Captain Edmond," Max the AI system answered!

The Zuruevians' exploration vessels were extremely agile; however, their designers neglected to develop a cloaking device to conceal their ships from radar detection systems and other trackers. When Azka entered Earth's atmosphere, he checked the planet's climate readings on his monitor and discovered there were places that were almost as cold as his planet year-round. As his spaceships descended toward the Artic Circle, Azka's face brightened with joy when he saw beautiful mountains and plains covered with snow. The sight of birds and animals fascinated the alien, who had never seen specific creatures as such. Through all his excitement, the explorer forgot proper procedure before activating the beacon and accidentally activated the homing device.

The discovery meant wealth and fame for his family, which was the prize promised to the one who discovered their new planet. After years of being cooped up inside the cockpit of his spaceship, Azka flew to Klinck Station, the coldest place on the world's largest island at -69.6⁰C. The alien crawled out of the vessel and could barely stand, hence he leaned against the ship for several minutes and recuperated. Even though their society was well protected from the fierce cold on Planet Zurue, the crunch of snow beneath his boots was heartwarming. Azka's home planet had similar atmosphere to Greenland's, hence his visor and helmet automatically retracted into the back of his space suit. Oxygen was the main chemical element they searched for across the universe, and the reason they had failed to find a home thus far. Zuruevians had never travelled to Earth, nevertheless some of their astronomers speculated the planet existed. While Azka basked in the coldness of the breeze, his ship's mainframe connected itself to multiple newscasts, social media sites, and government sites around the world, to determine who or what occupied the planet.

As he regained strength in his legs, Azka tried taking small steps away from the spaceship. After coming close to falling several times, the alien recaptured his form and could move about freely. The sensors on his ship could only detected the mammals and animals within a hundred miles, but Azka wanted to know more about the intellectual beings on the planet. With his interest peeking to discover more about Earth, the alien returned into the cockpit of his spaceship and began reviewing the information being collected.

When Junior Commandant Zonk of the Elite Flying Squad received Azka's homing alert, he was approaching the Andromeda Galaxy, which was 2.537 million lightyears away from Earth. Zonk felt skeptical about finding the livable planet they searched for somewhere within that galaxy, but once his onboard system received Azka's alert, the explorer ceased all search activities and blasted off towards Earth. Junior Commandant Zonk was in stasis while his spacecraft maneuvered towards its next planet of interest, but once the discovery alert was received, a mist of gas got expelled through the ventilation system. Once Zonk inhaled the gas and got awokened he began checking the vessel's monitor. The exploration vessel had already changed course and was speeding towards the discovered planet, therefore, Junior Commandant Zonk activated his message transponder.

"My Lord, a discovery alert was received! Request your approval to implement mission codename, Anarchy," Junior Commandant Zonk recorded then powered off the transponder?

During the voyage, 0.832 million lightyears later, Zonk's transponder began signalling the receipt of a message, to which he listened. "Your request has been granted, my pupil," responded his master!

With his request confirmed, the Elite Flying Squad commander increased the speed of his vessel to its maximum capacity. The exploration spaceship began moving through space at lightening speed, as it charged towards the Milky Way Galaxy. Rather than returning into stasis and allowing the vessel to pilot him to his destination, Junior Commandant Zonk decided to maintain control. Despite the great distance between Andromeda Galaxy and Earth's Milky Way, the two galaxies were quite visible from each other. The desire to complete his mission gave the commandant an adrenaline rush, thereby he assumed he could easily remain alert throughout the trip. However, sometime after he spoke with his master, Junior Commandant Zonk began dozing off with thoughts of his species being enslaved. Every elite astronaut had the same reoccurring nightmares, wherein they saw their families and comrades being enslaved, and their only saviour was Lord Ozar.

As the exploration vessel approached Planet Earth, the commandant got awakened before the warning alerts sounded. Zonk instantly began scanning the planet's surface to locate Azka's vessel, who was identified as Earth's locator. The spaceship's monitor could not provide a video feed of his comrade's vessel, but it did highlight Azka's flightpath. Once Junior Commandant Zonk located the ship, he charted a course to intercept the planet discoverer.

Azka left Greenland's airspace on route to Antarctica and flew across Baffin Bay, then the Northwestern Passages down into the north-eastern sections of Canada. The mammals, animals, birds, and fishes were creatures he had never seen before; therefore, he became fascinated by everything he saw. While approaching Axel Heiberg Island, the alien's warning sensor began illuminating. A few seconds later a pair of Canadian F-18 Fighter Jets settled in behind the exploration vessel and began pursuing it. The vessel's security system came online to help protect the alien, should the F-18 occupants begin an assault. The system also provided a video feed of both planes on a monitor, with a readout of their qualifications.

"There is no record of an aircraft like that in existence," Sergeant Logan Reacher reported!

"I never thought I would ever see something like that," Second Lieutenant James Crayguard said as he checked his instruments and opened a communication channel! "Bonjour, unidentified object! You are in violation of Canada's airspace! You are therefore ordered to follow us back to base or we will use excessive force!" The Canadian F-18 pilots waited a few seconds for a response; but got nothing in return.

"Do you think they heard you Second Lieutenant," Sergeant Reacher asked?

"According to my sensors they must have… Unidentified object, this is your last warning! Either you comply with the orders given or we will blow you out of the sky," Second Lieutenant Crayguard threatened as he armed his side missiles!

Once the exploration vessel detected the humans arming their weapons to fire, the spaceship sped away. Both F-18 pilots were shocked at the speed with which the spacecraft departed; however, they were ordered to intercept and apprehend the vessel. Despite the unidentified object's velocity, the human pilots thought their planes were fast enough to catch the alien and thereby took off in pursuit.

"Base command, this bogie is trying to evade capture," Sergeant Reacher exclaimed!

"Elaborate Sergeant," Colonel Dibbs responded!

"Colonel Dibbs, this unidentified craft is trying to get away, Sir," Sergeant Reacher reported!

"You are ordered to shoot that thing down, if necessary, Sergeant," Colonel Dibbs instructed!

"Copy that, Sir," Sergeant Reacher declared!

Draymond and Raymond were travelling so fast that the leg compressions built into their jet suits, compressed tighter to sustain the blood flow to their brains. Edmond had also installed vital sign monitors into the suits, to detect if any of his sons might faint. Even though Max would instantly take control if anything ever went astray, Edmond's priority was the safe health of his children, knowing Dee would kill him if they had an accident.

As they blasted over the tree ridges along the back country trails of British Columbia, Max transformed the car's windshield into an interactive screen, and began highlighting the chase between the Canadian Air Force pilots and Azka's alien vessel. It became immediately evident that the alien vessel was much faster and agile than the human aircrafts, as it sped away, then slowed down and waited, then finally sped away again. The twins could only laugh at watching the alien vessel make a mockery of the F-18s, which finally fired four missiles at the swift unidentified object. The spacecraft rocketed away from the missiles, as if they were walking during a race. Everything that the boys saw was also shown to Edmond, who could not believe what he was watching.

"Max, what is this," Edmond asked?

"Captain Edmond, this is an ongoing chase, several miles above our location," Max said!

"Max, what type of aircraft is the F-18s chasing and who made it," Edmond requested?

"Commander Edmond, there are no known answers to your question! That aircraft is not from Planet Earth," Max responded!

"How do you know it's not from this planet," Edmond asked?

"Captain, according to the airflow readings taken from the F-18, that ship is powered by a mineral that gives endless energy, but is not located here on Earth," Max explained!

"Wow! That was a spaceship from outer space? Like another planet," Raymond exclaimed?

"Yes, Pilot Raymond," Max responded!

"After seeing all that, you're joking right now, right? Dude, that thing was the fastest aircraft I've ever seen," Draymond argued!

As the twin boys watched the alien vessel distance itself from the F-18s, a Spec of Light dropped from above the clouds and blew off a section of the ship. None of the observers could believe what they had witnessed; therefore, they all began looking around for a second aircraft. Second Lieutenant Crayguard spun his F-18 to where he suspected the destructive shelling originated and caught sight of a similar vessel to the one sputtering to the ground. Before James could react, the vessel fired another Spec of Light that ripped off the left wing of his F-18. The jet immediately began sputtering to the ground; therefore, Second Lieutenant Crayguard pulled the emergency release handle and was ejected from the cockpit. Max enabled them to watch all the different action sequences on separate screens, hence they saw the air force pilot parachuted to the ground, but the alien went down with its spacecraft.

"Max, take us to the location where that spaceship just went down," Raymond instructed!

"As instructed, Pilot Raymond," Max stated before they change course!

Azka was knocked unconscious when the explosion occurred and became helpless during the descent. The on-board Orb was released from its operational port and inserted into Azka's spacesuit, where it took evasive actions to save his life. A second before the spacecraft crashed, his spacesuit bobbled him into a round ball, with an energy shield around him. When the ship crashed, the protective shield around Azka saved him from the fire and explosion that erupted, but he got thrown aside in the wreckage. When the 1963 Classic reached the crash site seconds later, they reduced speed and slowly drove through the fiery rubble.

"You guys be very careful, because something shot that thing down," Edmond warned!

"Over there! That looks like the pilot," Draymond then shouted!

"We have to go and check if it is still alive," Raymond exclaimed as he opened the door!

Both Draymond and Raymond exited the vehicle and slowly approached Azka. The twins were shocked to see the alien's anatomy still intact, following such a devastating crash. With Azka still irresponsive the Orb connected itself to their communication devices and spoke, "I am Azka from Planet Zurue. Please, help me?" The brothers dragged Azka to the car and placed him in the rear compartment behind their seats. Once they had secured the alien, the twins sped away from the crash site.

The Canadian pilots' base command knew the exact coordinates where their crashed airplane went down and had a rescue team on approach. Second Lieutenant Crayguard landed several meters away from the alien's crash site when he parachuted back to the ground. James could see the flames from both crashes yet was slightly more interested in recovering the debris and pilots from the alien ship. The Air Force pilot knew that his explanation of what happened could have gotten scrutinized, therefore, he began moving toward the spacecraft to secure whatever evidence he could find. While making his way to the site, James caught a quick glance of the fleeing vehicle, which flew by above the treelines.

Sergeant Reacher fired an unsuccessful missile at the object hidden behind the clouds, then realized it was moving towards him. After witnessing the destructive powers of the alien's spaceship, Logan who was further away from the vessel than Second Lieutenant Crayguard, quickly retreated. The alien wanted to ensure the humans were driven away from the area and therefore gave chase. Second Lieutenant Crayguard's report of his destroyed jet by an unidentified alien vessel infused Colonel Dibbs, who launched an additional seven jets, a Huey Helicopter and two Blackhawk Helicopters to reclaim sovereignty over Canadian airspace. When the alien vessel pursuing Sergeant Reacher's F-18 detected the incoming reinforcements, it quickly spun around and flew back toward the crash site. As the exploration spacecraft approached the area where Azka's vessel crashed, Junior Commandant Zonk targeted the destroyed ship's frame, and fired a Spec of Light that eradicated the remains. Second Lieutenant Crayguard was making his way toward the alien crash site when the explosion occurred. At the sound of the explosion the Air Force pilot crouched behind a tree to avoid being seriously injured by the blast, which wiped out a huge section of the woods.

Following the explosion, the Canadian pilot felt as though his had gone deaf, as his eardrums rang due to the loud blast. After the cloud of smoke and dust disappeared, Second Lieutenant Crayguard left from behind the tree disorientated, and walked pass another tree, to an area that was densely covered with pine trees prior. The Spec of Light fired by Junior Commandant Zonk had dug a huge crater, engulfed most of the trees in fire, and destroyed many others in the process. James stood at the ledge of the crater with an astonished look on his face, as he considered the destructive forces they might have to contend with.

"ey, you in there, can you hear me? Hello, are you still alive? Look at the size of this thing," Raymond asked while standing over Azka, who they laid on the garage floor!

"Can you stop bothering that thing in case it wakes up," Draymond declared?

"Do you think it can still breathe, Dad? I don't hear it inhaling or exhaling," Raymond remarked!

"What exactly did the alien voice say to you guys" Edmond asked?

"It said its name was Azka and then it asked us for help! But it hasn't said anything since," Draymond responded!

"Captain Edmond, this was what happened at the alien rescue location four seconds after we departed," Max reported while showing the video of the Spec of Light explosion on the computer screen.

"Wow, their species have some serious firepower! It seems like whosoever ambushed your friend here, tried to vanquish all the evidence! The question is why would it attack its own kind on a foreign planet," Edmond stated after seeing the results of the explosion!

"Maybe this guy was running away from him when the fighter jets showed up, Dad," Draymond speculated?

"I guess the only one who knows that answer, is your friend here. And for all we know, it could be a killer running away from justice," Edmond stated!

After the Orb got the humans to rescue its handler, the device disconnected its connection with the twin's communication system. Raymond had many questions he wanted answered and therefore kept trying to reconnect their link with the Orb. Due to the injury to its handler the Orb had to administer treatment through the spacesuit and neglected the humans thereafter. The Spec of Light that caused Azka's observation vessel to crash nearly killed him, thus he was still unconscious an hour later. The alien's spacesuit was in protective mode, so it was impossible to see its face through the visor attached to its helmet, check its pulse for life signs, or remove any of its armor. The Thornton's home phone unexpectedly rang with Dee calling to advise them 'she had arrived safely,' but the loud ringer visibly startled them all.

Once Junior Commandant Zonk destroyed Azka's exploration vessel, every spacecraft connected to his tracking device stopped in outer space. Without the broadcasting power built into every exploration spacecraft, the Orb that guided each Zuruevian explorer could not transmit the signal. After more than six years of cruising through space, everyone aboard the seven motherships felt overjoyed when their propulsion systems came online and the announcement of a 'tracking destination' was issued. Following years of uncertainty, the Zuruevians began celebrating their fortune, which quickly came to an abrupt stop. Back on the main transporter Emperor Zura summoned all his Council Members, the flight academy commanders, and their spaceship captains into a conference. All the spaceship captains and other invitees were transported onto the emperor's vessel, where he sought answers for what had happened. As soon as all the delegates were assembled inside the assembly hall, Emperor Zura entered and sat on his throne.

"Why have we stopped," Emperor Zura demanded?

Nobody could provide their ruler with a response to his question; therefore, they all lowered their heads.

"Chief Commander Ibik, these were your trainees! Why was our tracking disrupted," Emperor Zura asked?

"I have no idea what may have happened, Emperor Zura," Chief Commander Ibik responded!

"Emperor, maybe an alien block signal or destroyed our explorer," Council Member Four suggested?

"Emperor, if that should happen, it will only be a short time before another explorer locates this planet," Second Commander Xong declared!

"Zuruevians have waited years to find another home, and you expect them to wait longer, when they suspect we have located a planet," Emperor Zura stated?

"With all respects Emperor Zura, this was why I suggested we sent our more experienced pilot on this mission," Council Member Eight declared.

"Maybe those elders would still be searching, Council Member Eight," Second Commander Xong said!

"Enough! Do what you must and get us moving," Emperor Zura ordered before he exited!

"Yes, Emperor Zura," all the dignitaries responded!

Colonel Dibbs summoned Second Lieutenant Crayguard and Sergeant Reacher into his office for personal debriefing after their return. The medic on the rescue flight had to check Officer Crayguard's minor injuries, but he was cleared to resume his duties. The Air Force pilots' alien interaction was the talk of the base, especially after they measured the size of the crater. There was still a team of investigators at the crash site searching for fragments of the bomb or the alien ship, but they had not yet found anything.

"Gentlemen, I've gone over the video feed from your camcorders several times, and that was quite the experience! Now, I've got to report all this to our Prime Minister and several of our foreign allies in a few minutes. So, what are your thoughts of this whole ordeal," Colonel Dibbs asked?

"Colonel Sir, that thing went from zero to Mac-20 in less than three seconds, then pulled back up to us two seconds later! I've never seen anything that fast! Even when we fired our missiles at it, they were way too slow to catch that thing," Sergeant Reacher exclaimed!

"The only thing I know is that thing tried to kill me twice! Whatever those things were, we need to find a way to neutralize them right now, Sir," Second Lieutenant Crayguard argued!

"I agree with you Second Lieutenant, but how are we going to neutralize what we can't catch," Sergeant Reacher stated?

"Is it your belief that this foreign aircraft will travel even faster than our recorded speed," Colonel Dibbs asked?

"At the rate that aircraft maneuvered with ease! We have absolutely no doubt about that, Sir," Second Lieutenant Crayguard answered!

"Well, so far, our team on the ground have not found any evidence to take back to their lab for testing. But our satellites in the sky captured these images a few seconds before that bomb was dropped," Colonel Dibbs indicated as he began showing pictures of the Thornton twins rescuing Azka.

"Interesting, I knew I saw that car myself," Second Lieutenant Crayguard declared!

"If you think that was interesting, take a look at who it belongs to," Colonel Dibbs said!

"If it isn't my old buddy Edmond," Second Lieutenant Crayguard lamented!

Edmond made his sons refuel the car with jet fuel, while he searched military sites for information on the alien vessel. None of them were paying any attention to the alien, who sat upwards and began looking around the garage. Azka's helmet retracted into his spacesuit and made his head visible. Raymond was the first to notice their guest had awakened; however, he was stunned to see the alien's actual features.

"Dad, dad! That thing is awake," Raymond stated!

Edmond signalled the boys to move closer to him, as he was unsure of what would happen. Azka realized he could not fully stand due to the height of the roof, so he remained seated on the floor. Neither of the twins were wearing their flight helmets, therefore the Orb connected with Max to communicate.

"Thank you, Earthlings, for saving me! I mean you no harm," Max spoke!

"Who are you and where did you come from," Edmond asked?

"I am Azka, Explorer 30! From Planet Zurue," Azka stated!

"Why did you come here to Earth," Edmond questioned?

"Planet Zurue was destroyed. I seek to find new planet for my species," Azka responded.

"Why did another spaceship destroy your ship," Edmond asked?

"I have no response. Nor can I revive beacon, without my ship. My mission has failed," Azka explained!

"Dad, it sounds like he needs a high-powered satellite to transmit his signal," Draymond whispered.

"I heard him son! I'm just not sure we can trust him," Edmond whispered back.

"I trust him, Dad, and we need to help him! Whosoever shot down his spaceship obviously wanted to stop him from completing his mission," Raymond exclaimed!

"My sensors have detected four military helicopters with armed soldiers on-board, three minutes away," Max reported, therefore, Azka changed positions and knelt on one knee!

"Ok, son! If that's what you think we should do! Azka, I think it is time for you to introduce yourself to the world; besides, we need to make them capture us for this plan to work," Edmond declared!

"Dad, no! You can't let them take you, there must be another way," Draymond quarreled!

"Son, I worked with those people for years, so I know how they operate! I want you boys to leave and use Max to help find us later tonight! My guess is they might bring us to Chilliwack Base for interrogation and examination, which is perfect because they have a powerful enough satellite there, we can use to send that signal," Edmond declared!

"What if something goes wrong and we can't find you, or they separate the two of you," Raymond asked?

"Don't worry about it, I will find a way to convince them that I am the only person who understands our friend here! But we do whatever we have to do, like always," Edmond replied!

"Ok, Dad," Raymond answered!

"Earthling Edmond, please allow me to help? Permit my Orb to merge with your transportation's on-board system for performance enhancement," Azka's Orb requested?

The thought of their vehicle exceeding its maximum capabilities excited Edmond who calmly responded, "Go right ahead!"

"Request confirmed! Connecting to vehicle's A.I system... Connected," stated the alien Orb!

The data on Edmond's laptop began flashing before the screen went blank.

"Max," called Edmond as the screen returned!

"I am your new on-board advisor, Max-X," sounded the response through the vehicle's speakers!

"Let me get that key? It's my turn to drive," Raymond declared as he grabbed the key from Draymond!

The twins climbed into the car as the garage door opened. It was dark outdoors and difficult to see beneath the tree shadows, therefore they flew off and maintained a close distance to the road's surface. To take advantage of the darkness, Max-X featured their route on the screen, while they sped along without headlights. Despite the soldiers' alertness, the modified classic car passed under one of the choppers without anyone on-board noticing.

A few seconds after the 63 Classic left, spotlights from the Huey Helicopters lit up the garage exterior, while soldiers descended from ladders into the yard. Nearly forty Special Ops soldiers surrounded the garage and took up evasive positions. The soldiers chose to proceed with caution due to the alien's firepower capabilities; therefore, they were hesitant to rush inside. Second Lieutenant Crayguard and Sergeant Reacher tagged along with the apprehension team, to get their first views of the alien. With the garage lit up bright and all the soldiers aiming their rifles at the structure, Special Operative, Major Demitry Dilo spoke through a loudspeaker.

"Doctor Edmond Thornton, this is Major Demitry Dilo with the Canadian Special Ops Division! We are here to take you and your guest into custody; and would like to achieve our objective without any hostilities! Now we know that your two sons are in there with you, along with their friend they offered a ride, who we would very much like to talk with! I'm sure you understand Doctor, that we must find out why he's here; so, we can keep the rest of our society safe! So, Doctor Thornton, we are going to need all of you to come out with all your hands held high, or we will be forced to use aggression!"

Major Dilo then waited two minutes for the occupants to surrender, but nobody came out. All the soldiers grew increasingly nervous about attacking the alien, whom they assumed carried some sort of vaporizing weapon. Regardless of their fears, their orders were to capture the alien at any cost, therefore if every other option failed, they would have to storm the garage.

"Doctor Thornton, you are leaving us with no other alternative than to come…" Major Dilo began!

"Hold on Major, let me try and talk to him," Second Lieutenant Crayguard asked, to which Major Dilo passed him the speaker? "Hey Edmond, this is your old friend James Crayguard! We had a little run in with your alien friend today, so these guys are here on national security business. Edmond, I don't want anything to happen to you or your family, so I think it's best if you guys do as Major Dilo says!"

Inside the garage Edmond and Azka watched the soldiers on the surveillance feed, being provided by the outdoor cameras. Following Second Lieutenant Crayguard's plea, Edmond took a canister of acid and poured it all over his laptop, which short-circuited and caught fire. The burning laptop was the soldiers' first positive indication that the garage was occupied. Seconds later the garage door slowly opened at which Edmond and Azka exited with their hands held high.

Junior Commandant Zonk returned to the realm of space where he activated the device given to him back on Planet Zurue. The device was a low frequency transmitter that could be detected and tracked by members of his elite flying squad who were within 1.87 million lightyears of his location. A controversial Zuruevian astronomer who believed there were other species out in the universe, had long suspected there was an inhabited planet somwhere in the Virgo Supercluster of galaxies. The astronomer's speculations were never validated, yet there were government separatists who adhered to his rhetoric. When the exploration missions were being issued, six elite astronauts got assigned to that sector and the surrounding galaxies. Contrary to the Elite flyers, Azka discovered the Milky Way Galaxy by luck and outdid those who were given actual coordinates by which to search. After the final explorer blasted off into space, Azka took one final look at the planet, before he turned his vessel into the direction with the least number of glowing stars.

With the other five elite explorers within proximity, Junior Commandant Zonk expected their arrivals within the coming days. The wait for his associates gave Zonk the time to study Earth's habitants and their different forms of living. Like his species, many earthlings lived under monarchies, communist, and dictatorship regimes, yet he had never known of a democratic society, where residents were free to do as they wished. The people of Earth also did weird things that fascinated Zonk, such as worshiped different gods and gathered to pray. Despite being worshipers, earthlings were not immune to wars and fighting, in fact there were many places where conflicts raged on. As Junior Commandant Zonk studied the people of Earth, he realized that for them to conquer the planet, their species would engage in warfare for many generations.

Hiding in outer space also gave the commandant the chance to remain off planetary radars, wherein humans could not easily trace his actual location. Their mission was on schedule and expected to last several years; before they were instructed to reinstate the beacon for the others to track. After years of being cooped up inside his explorer vessel, Junior Commandant Zonk was eager to lay his feet on the planet, but he had to remain disciplined and follow the mission's course. The sights of Earth from space, the sounds, the life forces, and everything he witnessed made Earth the perfect home, therefore the alien grew increasingly jealous of the humans who resided there.

The Special Operatives team brought Edmond and Azka to Canadian Forces Base Chilliwack, like the paralyzed ex-astronaut predicted. While Edmond was permitted to drive himself about in his wheelchair, Azka was subdued with a unique form of handcuff. There were extra security personnel on hand to secure the base and ensure the alien captive did not escape. After the soldiers took Edmond and Azka into custody, they searched the rest of the property for Raymond and Draymond. With the twins not being a priority, the soldiers departed once they extinguished the laptop fire, boarded their prisoners, and searched the rest of the premises.

When they reached the base, the soldiers unexpectedly separated Edmond and Azka and brought the alien to their most remotely secured building. Edmond quarrelled that he was the only one capable to translate for the Zuruevian, but Second Lieutenant Crayguard and Major Dilo ignored him. The soldiers brought Edmond into the administrative building, where they left him to wait for the investigators inside a room. Nearly five minutes later a Lieutenant Perremen and another officer entered the room, fully dressed for combat.

"Doctor Thornton, I am Lieutenant Perremen sent to take your statement about what happened! I guess this must be an uncomfortable situation for you," Lieutenant Perremen stated?

"Where have they taken the alien? I told that Major Dilo I was the only person who could translate for Azka, yet still they have me locked inside this room," Edmond exclaimed!

"Azka, so that's his name? Don't worry about the alien, our national security team will get the information they want from him sooner or later! Let's talk about what happened during the time he was inside your garage, what did he reveal to you about why he came here," Lieutenant Perremen questioned?

"Azka said he is an explorer," Edmond answered.

"So, what planet is he from," Lieutenant Perremen asked?

"Listen, we're wasting quality time! For all I know there could be an invasion coming," Edmond exclaimed!

"What! You mean like aliens attacking us," Lieutenant Perremen franticly asked?

With Azka's spacesuit within the Canadian Forces Base Chilliwack compound, the difficulties for Max-X logging into the security system were minimal. The Orb connected itself to the on-base computer system, which enabled the twins to view every area of the compound through their camera systems. Max-X provided visual and audio recordings of Edmond and Azka, who were being held in separate facilities on the base. Azka's spacesuit was being stored inside a storage compartment; within the same structure they imprisoned him. The video of Azka was disturbing to the twins, but they had to wait until circumstances changed on the base, before they risked attempting to rescue the alien and their father. While Raymond and Draymond focused on what was transpiring on the screen, Max-X located the building, the operation's room, and the precise computer needed to transmit the tracking signal.

"I thought dad said they would stay together," Raymond argued?

"Relax bro, it's still early! Things could change," Draymond answered!

"What do you mean relax? It's already a disaster! How are we supposed to rescue them now," Raymond said?

"Calm down bro, it's not that deep! Whatever happens we'll work it out," Draymond related.

"What the heck was dad thinking? Dude, that's a military base, they could lock us up like forever, even shoot us," Raymond quarrelled!

"Bro, if you're scared, just say so! I'll go in and get them myself," Draymond suggested!

"I'm not scared! I'm just saying, that's a military base, and they have soldiers, with big guns, so, that's all I'm saying," Raymond responded.

"So, you're scared then," Draymond teased?

"Dude, shut up! I ain't the one who's scared of bugs! You are," Raymond fired back!

"Whatever," Draymond exclaimed!

Azka's spacesuit and clothing were removed, before the soldiers strung him up with metal braces around his wrists and ankles. The braces were magnetically connected to an energizing machine, that held the alien suspended in midair. The humans could administer electrical shocks through the metal braces, to stun their captives or knock them unconscious. While the alien hung inside the empty chamber, two doctors entered and examined him by withdrawing fluid samples, checked his temperature, and took pictures. Moments later the doors again slid open, at which Colonel Dibbs, Sergeant Reacher, Major Dilo, Second Lieutenant Crayguard, and a language expert walked into the chamber.

"Before we begin, I'm not sure if you understand me or not, but this remote here in my hand will be used to cause you some discomfort if we suspect that you are not being truthful to us," Major Dilo threatened before he pressed the button that gave Azka an electric shock!

"Ahhhhh," Azka yelled in pain!

"Now that you have gotten the message! Who are you and why have you come to my planet," Major Dilo demanded?

Azka stared at the military personnels with contempt, then spoke in his native tongue to try and force his interrogators to summon his friend Edmond. "I am Azka from Planet Zurue, I mean you no harm!"

After Azka responded, Major Dilo and the others looked at the translator, who shook his head to stipulate there was no Earthly translation for the Zuruevian language. Major Dilo thought the alien knew another language and was lying to them, therefore he pressed the electrocution button and held it for several seconds. "I think you are lying to us; and you know some other ways to communicate!"

The pain was intense and forced the alien to murmur, "Ahhhh!"

"Major Dilo, that's enough! We need answers, so go and get Doctor Thornton over here, if he understands this thing," Colonel Dibbs ordered!

"Yes, Sir," Major Dilo answered before he exited the chamber!

When Edmond got transferred to the security facility, he drove his motorized wheelchair into the main lobby where Colonel Dibbs, Second Lieutenant Crayguard, Sergeant Reacher, and another officer were waiting. Prior to joining the astronaut program, Edmond worked for the National Defense Department, therefore he was aware of their procedures. Both Edmond and Second Lieutenant Crayguard despised each other since they were cadets, but the hatred mounted when Edmond got selected to become an astronaut and James' application was refused. Lieutenant Perremen went over to Colonel Dibbs and whispered something to him, which seemed to anger the base commander.

"Doctor Thornton, how have you been since your retirement," Colonel Dibbs asked?

"Taking it one day at a time, Colonel," Edmond answered!

"Well Doctor, I'm not sure if you are aware, but another vessel like the one your garage guest came here in, shot down his spaceship and one of my F-18 jets! That spaceship then proceeded to blast a huge crater in the B.C back country, before it took off and flew away! Apparently, hadn't your sons rescued their garage guest, that thing would have been dead. Still, I could care less about that creature, I just want to know why they brought their fight here on Earth," Colonel Dibbs stated?

"It took me a few hours to understand how Azka communicate, but I can translate, Colonel," Edmond declared.

"Very well, the government has a few questions they want answered. So, if you could do us the honors Doctor Thornton," Colonel Dibbs asked as he guided Edmond toward the holding facility?

When they entered the chamber where they imprisoned Azka, and Edmond saw the degrading manner with which they subdued the alien, he quickly devised a plan to get the visitor released. Colonel Dibbs had taken the electrocution device from Major Dilo and held it in his hand.

"Colonel, these alien beings have the ability to connect telepathically with humans, so unless we are two feet away from each other, this is not going to work," Edmond explained.

"Get that alien released! Then I want everybody out; only Doctor Thornton gets left with that thing," Colonel Dibbs ordered!

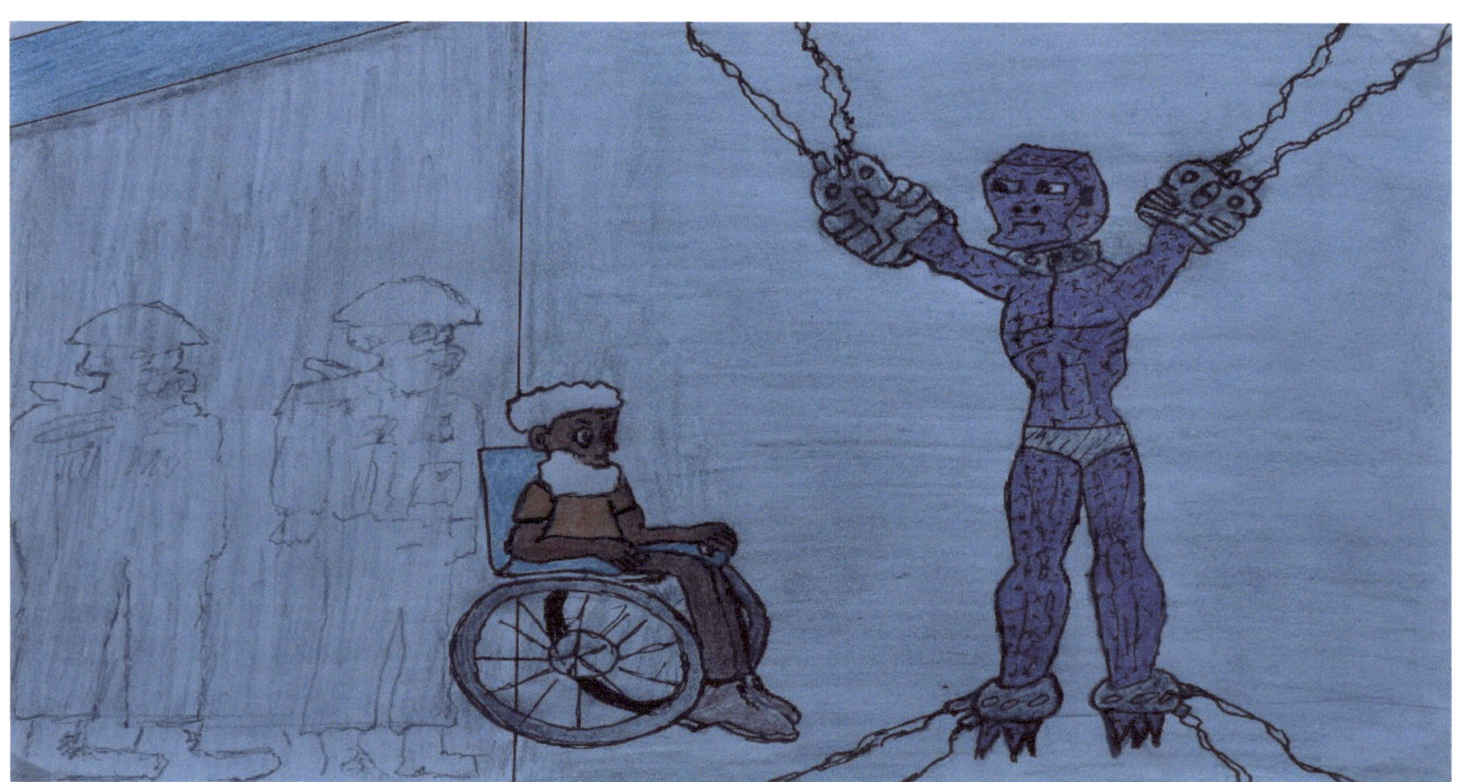

The guards locked off the power source to Azka's magnetic restraints, which made him fall to the floor and abled to move freely about the chamber. Edmond knew they could not communicate without Azka's spacesuit, nevertheless he had to convince their observers they were being genuine. The completion of their mission required that they transmit the signal to the Zuruevian vessels, therefore they had to get rid of the interrogators. Azka was incredibly irate about the treatment he had received, so it took Edmond a few minutes to calm him down. Once the alien became less temperamental, Edmond motioned him to sit on a chair for them to talk.

Colonel Dibbs and the rest of officers monitored the interaction between Edmond and the alien from the observation room next door. Azka knew what they were there to accomplish, therefore although they could not understand each other, he knew to follow Edmond's lead. Although he had no idea what was taking place, the alien followed Edmond's hand signals, and sat across from him while they maintained eye contact. Once Edmond felt they had convinced the observers they were telepathically linked, he signalled Colonel Dibbs with a thumbs up.

"What is his name and what planet did he travel here from," Colonel Dibbs asked?

"He said they mean us no harm! His name is Azka an explorer; and his home was called Planet Zurue," Edmond answered.

"Why did he travel here to our planet," Colonel Dibbs questioned?

"His species seek a new home, after their planet imploded," Edmond stated.

"If they meant us no harm, why did his associate shoot down my F-18 Jet," Colonel Dibbs demanded?

"He said he has no answers to your question Colonel," Edmond remarked.

"Is he expected to report the planets he found," Colonel Dibbs asked?

"He said his report was already issued! The rest of his species are coming," lied Edmond!

The false disclosure had the exact effect Edmond thought it would, when Colonel Dibbs abruptly ended their discussion, and marched from the facility with his observers following.

The entire compound at Canadian Forces Base Chilliwack was incredibly silent at 1:12am, when the 63 Classic sped over the western fence and hovered above the facility where Azka and Edmond were imprisoned. The vehicle slowly descended onto the roof, while the tires dismounted from their holding compartments. Once the vehicle got parked, Raymond and Draymond exited the flying car wearing their headphone and ear-pods, to acquire instructions and communicate with Max-X. The Orb had taken control of the base's security system, wherein it provided access to any door the twins needed to enter. To conceal every action the twins made, the Orb disrupted each video recording they passed.

Both young men were eager to get their father and friend out of lockup, so they moved about quickly on their hovering skateboards. The Orb unlocked the door to the roof and gave the twins instructions on exactly where to go. Once they entered the facility and made their way to the ground level by use of the service stairs, the Orb separated the twins and sent Draymond to recuperate Azka's spacesuit. While his brother went to the storage area, Raymond got sent to the holding facility, which had to be opened from the exterior by imputing a numeric code. The facility was empty by then and the guards were outside the building protecting the parameter.

There were two cots provided for both prisoners to rest, so Edmond and Azka were laying down staring up at the ceiling. When the confinement doors began opening, both prisoners had no idea what to expect, until Raymond rushed into the chamber. Throughout their interactions, the Orb maintained the same video feed of the prisoners relaxing on their cots. With only a short window with which to finalize their mission, the prisoners hugged and hurried from the chamber. Draymond recovered the spacesuit from storage and met the others inside the lobby. The alien used his brute strength and snapped off the metal braces around his wrists and ankles; before he got dressed in his spacesuit. Rather than taking the stairs the Orb directed them to an elevator, to transport them to the top floor. Azka was much taller than the height of the elevator, hence he was forced to crouch and bend his knees to fit inside. The facility where they were held was not a prison, therefore the guards were not expected to make regular checks on the detainees. All four escapees exited the building through the roof's emergency door, then climbed into the vehicle, which was a bit of a tight squeeze. Raymond and his brother allowed their father and Azka to occupy the front compartment, while they sat in the back with the wheelchair and their hoverboards.

When the 1963 Classic landed on the telecommunication building's roof top, Edmond chose to accompany Azka on the beacon mission. Although it was a simple task, Edmond wanted to ensure the alien was not deceiving them. There was nobody detected inside the building, so both escapees spoke candidly as they moved through the hallways. The Orb had disabled the alarm system, provided them entry into the building, and awarded access into restricted areas. To conceal both their identities the device sabotaged the video feeds as they moved throughout the secured building. The Operation's Room where the main computer system for the base's satellite was on the second floor, therefore the Orb guided them to that location.

"So, what type of a society was Planet Zurue? Does your species have a ruler or was it a democratic society," Edmond asked?

"Zuruevians have what Earthlings call, emperor," Azka answered.

"What was the name of your emperor," Edmond asked?

"Emperor Zura," Azka responded!

"Why do you Zuruevians have feathers all over their bodies," Edmond asked?

"My planet very cold. Feathers keep Zuruevians warm," Azka stated!

"How long does your Orb estimate before your ships receive the signal," Edmond enquired?

"Orb estimate signal could take up to sixty Earthling years," Azka answered.

When they reached the Operation's Room and approached the main computer station, Azka retracted the Orb from its holding compartment. The alien proceeded to place the device next to the computer, while Edmond powered up the system. It took the alien technology eight seconds, before Azka recuperated the device and returned it to its holding compartment. Edmond and Azka safely entered and exited one of the most secured buildings at Canadian Forces Base Chilliwack, before they climbed back aboard the 1963 Classic and left the compound.

Colonel Dibbs had been on a live video conference since he abruptly departed from the observation chamber and went directly to his office. The video feed originally began with his commander, General Cid Talpot, who then linked his Chief of The Defense Staff, Aniel Gernip, who in turn connected the Prime Minister and the Chief of the Armed Forces. Each of the government officials contacted wanted to see verification of the alien, therefore Colonel Dibbs provided the live video footage from inside the holding facility. Although the officials saw visual evidence of the alien, they all advised the colonel they would be adjusting their schedules to visit the base for a more indept view. Once Colonel Dibbs debriefed them about the bombing incident, then informed them of what he had learnt about the Zuruevian Species relocating to Earth, their conversation expanded even wider.

With such excitement and uncertainty about the alien and his species coming to Earth, Sergeant Reacher and Second Lieutenant Crayguard chose to remain on the base. Despite the late hour, none of the soldiers inside their barracks could sleep comfortably, with such uncertainty about their future. Major Dilo had Sergeant Reacher and Second Lieutenant Crayguard inside his personal quarters sharing a bottle of Scotch. The officers had spent years in the Canadian Armed Forces, during which they encountered many threats, yet they all feared what was to come. The sole conversation ongoing throughout the compound, was whether mankind would need to go to war against aliens for control of Earth.

The guards throughout the compound thought their detainees were safely locked inside their secured prison. The video cameras inside the holding room showed both detainees on their cots, from the moment everyone vacated the facility. At 1:45am a guard entered the holding structure to gather information on their detainees' choices for breakfast. Once the guard used his security card to gain access into the building, the video feed inside the holding room changed. As soon as the guard who monitored the security video screens throughout the compound saw the empty cell, she immediately initiated the escape alarm.

"Where are they," Colonel Dibbs demanded after he returned to the facility and saw it empty?

"We have no idea, Sir! I have our men searching the entire building," answered Major Dilo!

"How did they manage to walk out of here without anybody seeing them, huh," Colonel Dibbs demanded?

"The only other way out of here is by some sort of alien transport, Colonel," Major Dilo responded!

Six Earthly days after Junior Commandant Zonk activated the low frequency homing device, he reunited with his first fellow Zuruevian. Kuvu's spaceship slowed from warp speed when the vessel got within five miles of Earth, before it cruised to a stop beside Junior Commandant Zonk's explorer. Neither Zuruevian had seen an intellectual being since they departed from Planet Zurue, yet they only looked at each other expressionless for a second, then refocused their attention on their activities. The powerful mind control, their master had over his Elite students, protruded them from expressing any sentiments to friends, family, and even teammates. Their academy commanders had been unknowingly reprograming their minds since they joined the flight program, therefore, none of them were their actual selves.

Three days later Zorv arrived and rejoined his mates, however contrary to Zonk and Kuvu he refrained from acknowledging anyone. Each new arrival illustrated the effects of being in a solitary confined space for a duration of time, while constantly envisioning the same tragic thoughts. The last Elite Flyers arrived twenty-five days after Junior Commandant Zonk activated the low frequency homing device. With his mini command strike force assembled, Zonk, followed procedure, and played a prerecorded video of Lord Ozar, issuing their orders. Each of the Elite Flyers watched the recording on their monitors inside their cockpits.

"Congratulations my pupils! You have done well, yet this is only the first step to fulfilling my master plan! This Planet Earth; was long spoken of by the teacher, as a world infested with racist barbarians! For you and your families to have a future on this planet, there must be tyranny! Find an appropriate location for our landing; and stake our claim," Lord Ozar instructed at which the message abruptly ended!

Junior Commandant Zonk had been in Earth's orbit longer than his associates, yet he had neglected to educate himself on the planet's geological landscape. Rather than initially locating the perfect place to live, Zonk, got caught up watching video highlights relating to government, social, and political issues across the globe. As leader of the squad, it was his duty to select the best location to capture, therefore Zonk retraced Azka's flight path, which navigated back to Greenland. The commandant assumed that Azka had chosen the location, therefore he plotted a course for Earth's largest island. All the elite flyers ignited their engines, then blasted off as a unit towards the planet's surface.

"**Y**es Honey, I understand the Feds have been harassing you; and I'm sorry you have to be on vacation with the police parked across the street from your parents' house, watching you! But we have a global problem, we're trying to sort out," Edmond argued via Max-X's connection inside the garage!

"I don't cares what you need do to get them police from round my parents' yard, but you better do it A-sap," Dee quarrelled!

To get a bit of privacy from his sons and Azka, Edmond locked himself inside the 63 Classic. "But Honey, I can't work miracles! Right now, we have to hide out, until we figure out our next move!"

The Thornton men and their alien friend were at a two-bedroom house several miles from Wabamun Lake, in Duffield, Alberta. The residence was built for a tall family; therefore, the roof was high enough for Azka to move about safely. Every facet of the house was modern, hence the garage connected to the main house and was accessible through a door. Draymond went and sat inside the days room, where he began watching television while he played with his videogaming consul. Azka was quite interested in earthlings' day to day activities, so he walked into the house and stood by watching the twins.

"Hey Az, you good? Do you drink water or eat our type of food," Raymond asked while eating an apple and wearing his headphones?

"Yes Raymond, I am good! I have never tried Earthling food. What is that on your head," Azka said?

"Oh, these my headphones, we listen to music through them," Raymond answered as he removed them and placed them over the alien's head!

"Is this music," Azka asked?

"Yeah, almost every culture here has their own music! Don't your species have music or entertainment," Raymond enquired?

"I have never heard of this music! What do you do with this music," Azka stated?

"Dude, you dance to it, like this," Raymond answered as he busted a move!

"Bro, you call that dancing," Draymond exclaimed before he got up and started doing his personal dance?

Azka saw a videogame consul in Draymond's hand and grew curious. "What is that Draymond?"

"Oh, this is my videogame consul! We play games on them, for entertainment," Draymond said!

"What is this games," Azka asked?

"Look," Draymond answered and began illustrating how the device worked! "Haven't you played video games before?"

Azka thought back to his childhood and became saddened when he thought of all the things he missed growing up. The alien's head dropped as he turned away to avoid facing the twins. "Because of danger to Planet Zurue and exploration mission; I had very little childhood!"

"How old were you when you left Planet Zurue on the mission," Raymond asked?

"I was almost twelve of Earthling years," Azka declared.

"And how long have you been alone in space," Raymond questioned?

"Eleven years, ten months and six days of your Earthling time," Azka responded!

"That means you only a few years older than us," Raymond sighted.

Draymond noticed a Special Alert warning on the television, which featured aircraft carrier ships at sea and military fighter jets flying about in the sky. The highlight also showed several Zuruevian exploration vessels flying around a country's territory. Once Draymond saw the spaceships, he turned up the television volume to listen to the reporter's comments.

"Dad, dad," Draymond shouted at which Edmond rushed into the house!

"…military officials have told us they knew of these aliens for weeks now and have been tracking them, but nobody knows what sparked this latest conflict, where we now have six confirmed alien spaceships, circling Greenland at rapid speeds," the reporter commented!

"This is terrible, because any conflict could lead to our first intergalactic war, when your emperor gets here," Edmond stated!

Back on Emperor Zura's main transporter, the system detected the signal sent from Earth. When the main operator's deck received the alert, they were suspicious of the homing beacon due to the frequency, but they had to bring the matter to the emperor. For every major decision the entire governing council were obligated to meet, therefore all the emperor's advisors gathered inside his conference hall. Since the tracking interruption occurred, many of the Zuruevian citizens had begun inciting ideas of corruption. Everyone had been nervously eager for another tracking symbol; however, to avoid infusing his naysayers Emperor Zura ordered his cabinet members to keep all government business private. Regardless of his efforts, false news about the emperor's involvement in the tracking stoppage kept circulating aboard the different ships and plummeted his approval ratings.

When Emperor Zura entered the conference hall where his loyal advisors were gathered, he observed that there were four of his counselors who refrained from bowing their heads. Even though the emperor spent most of his time secluded in his personal section of the ship, he had heard the rumors circulating about his failing their species. Emperor Zura walked over to his highchair and sat, then signalled his ship's captain to present his report.

"Emperor Zura, our system has detected a foreign tracking signal," Captain Uraq reported!

"Where does it lead," Council Member 11 asked?

"In the same direction we were traveling previously," Captain Uraq answered!

"This is a trick, Emperor Zura! We must wait until we receive Zuruevian contact," Council Member 8 said!

"I agree with the council member, we should wait for Zuruevian contact. What if this false signal takes us light-years away from a true discovery," Lord Ozar declared?

Emperor Zura considered the escalating revolt against his government and thought it best if Zuruevians knew they were heading to a destination, therefore he responded, "We shall pursue this tracking signal!"

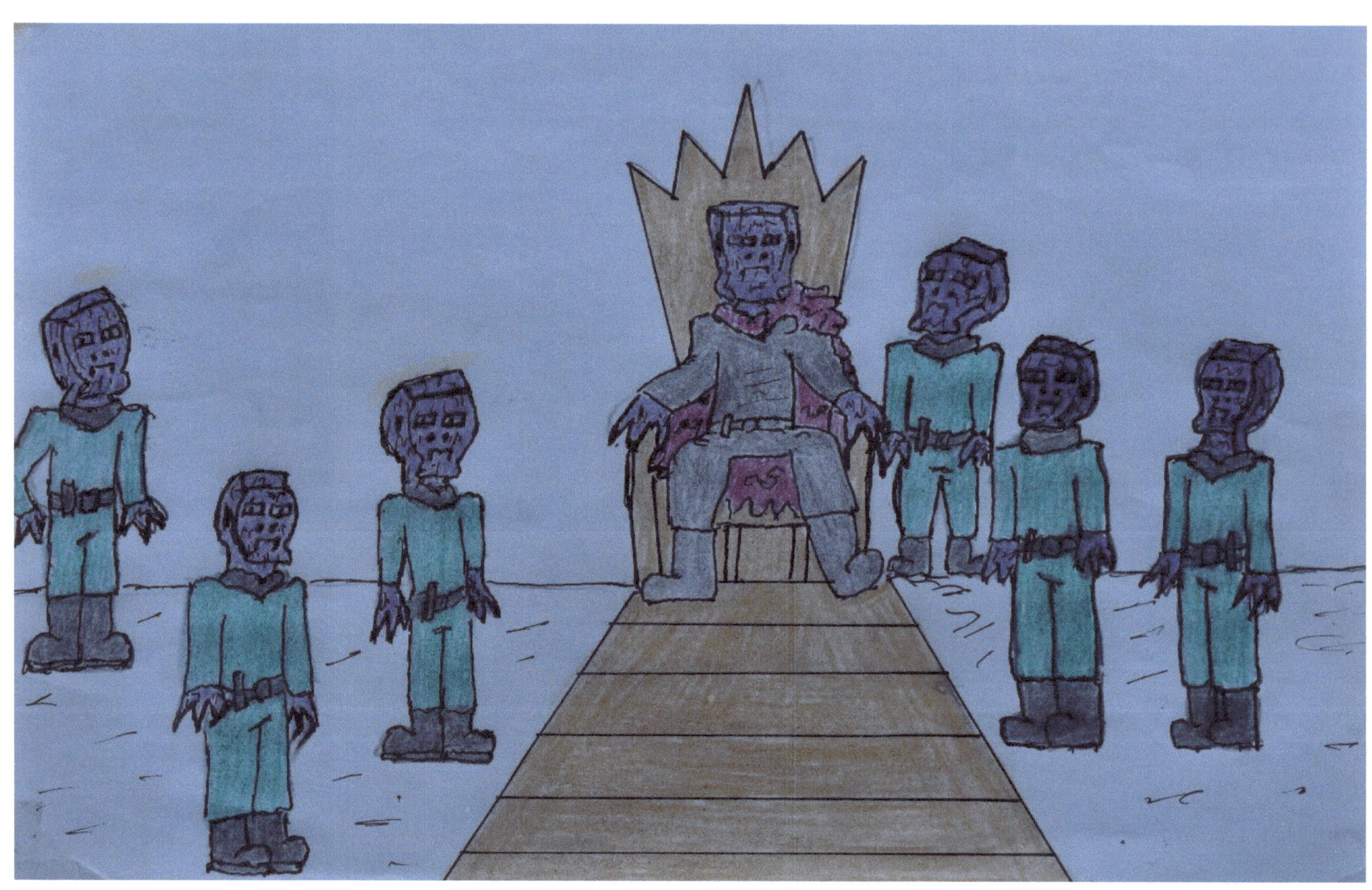

Two days later an emergency meeting was called between the Kingdom of Denmark and every major leader around the globe. With such a threat to mankind's sovereignty, rulers worldwide wanted to know if the Zuruevians were beginning their conquest of Earth. Despite several major ongoing conflicts between certain leaders, concerned rulers poured into the United Nations Building in Geneva, Switzerland, solely to discuss the aliens' course of action. There had been no communications made by the aliens, who continued to circle Greenland and impeded every vehicle from entering the airspace. Once Denmark's military began closely surveying the exploration vessels, they determined that each spaceship was circling Greenland, at a ratio of thirty-five times per minute. The estimated 56, 650 residents who lived in places such as Nuuk, Qaqortoq, and Qaanaaq, became fearsome for their lives and locked themselves inside their residences. Even though Greenland belonged to the Kingdom of Denmark, a worldwide invasion would eventually include other countries, therefore every ruler attended to have their say.

"Ladies and gentlemen, this emergency meeting of the United Nation General Assembly is now underway! Our first report is from Colonel Dibbs of the Canadian Forces," U.N Chairman Pout said!

"Good morning! The Canadian Air Force intercepted an alien spacecraft inside Canadian airspace almost a month age. When we tried apprehending this spacecraft, we learnt this vessel was way faster than our fighter jets." Colonel Dibbs' female assistant began showing images on the big screen of the exploration vessel being pursued by the F-18 Jets. "As you all can see from the video footage, this spacecraft was extremely fast and did unconventional things while at high speed. Even when my pilots tried to take it down with their missiles, that thing outran the bombs, can't say I've ever seen anything do that in all my years of service! Later here in the video, you see another spacecraft just beyond the clouds, firing two precisely guided strikes which took out the first spaceship and one of our F-18 Fighter Jets. These final images were taken from the International Space Station several seconds later; and show this spacecraft returning to the crash site, where it did this!" The audience members gasped at the sight of the crater, after being impressed by the agility of the spaceship.

"Who are these aliens and why do they threaten Greenland," Prime Minister Gorquu of Greenland asked?

"Mr. Prime Minister, we know they are a species known as the Zuruevians! We also know their entire…" Colonel Dibbs began before his microphone went dead and Junior Commandant Zonk appeared on the large video screen.

"Earthlings, Greenland now belongs to the Confederation of Zurue," Zonk threatened then terminated the link!

A fleet of sixteen war ships and aircraft carriers surrounded Greenland from the north in the Lincoln Sea, the west in Baffin Bay, east along the Artic Ocean, and to the south in the Labrador Sea. The ships were owned by Denmark, America, Russia, China, England, and Canada, most of whom disagreed on how the alien matter should be handled. While Denmark only sought the best approach to getting their people and territory released, the other countries differed on whether it should be done diplomatically or by force. Several military strategists believed they could jointly shoot down the spacecrafts regardless of the speed they travelled, but others speculated that the aliens could go much faster.

Regardless of their disagreement on how to proceed, the countries all recognized that if war should occur, they would have to combine forces to deal with the aliens. Those who thought it best to use diplomatic methods, pointed to the fact that none of them knew what they were up against, therefore they should wait until the ideal representatives arrived. Without the ability to contact the aliens, people were fearsome it would take years before their representatives arrived, so many supported shooting down the spaceships. As the agonizing days went by those seeking a diplomatic solution to the possible crisis, kept praying for a peaceful solution. People like the pope and archbishops around the world held daily prayer vigils to help strengthen the nations, but everyone knew it was only a matter of time before something happened.

On the fifth day of the conflict Denmark issued its first formal warning to the Confederation of Zurue via satellite, news channels, and social media platforms, where they announced, "We are prepared to shoot down your spaceships if you do not vacate Greenland's territory!" Reports showed the aliens heard the warning but chose to remain silent. Five days later Denmark issued its second threat where they warned, "To the Confederation of Zurue, you have five days to leave Greenland's territory, or we will shoot down your spaceships!" Again, the aliens remained silent until the fourth day, where they responded to the message via satellite, "We Zuruevians do not fear you!" Five days thereafter the Kingdon of Denmark repositioned all the big guns on their war ships and aimed them at the flightpaths being taken by the aliens. With their big guns pointed at the spaceships the government issued their third warning where they said in the message, "Our weapons are prepared to shoot down your spaceships unless you vacate Greenland's territory immediately!" Still the Zuruevians ignored all the threats and continued circling Greenland.

Azka sat before the television and watched every second of broadcasting provided by the major news stations and the Canadian Naval Forces. As he watched the developments, he thought back to the night he overheard Junior Commandant Zonk and his master. Although he had no idea what their ultimate motive was, he knew he was the only one who had any notion of their secret plot. There was nothing else he could have done without risking being killed or getting his new friends locked in prison, yet it pained Azka to sit and watch the developing tension.

The twins became concerned for their friend who watched the newsfeed for eight straight days, until he passed out and slept for twenty-two hours. After he woke rather than getting into his spacesuit for nutrition, which was how they got fed out in space, Azka went right back to watching the newscast for another eight days. Raymond and Draymond felt they needed to do something to help their friend, but none of them could think of a way that would be impactful. Several days later while watching the newsfeed, Draymond went over and sat beside Azka. Edmond was on the phone speaking with Dee, who was supposed to return home days before, but understood her family's predicament and extended her stay in Trinidad and Tobago.

"How you doing Az," Draymond sympathetically asked?

"Azka not doing good Draymond," the alien responded!

"Didn't you have any other friends at that flight school, apart from that jerk Commandant Zonk," Draymond asked?

After days of watching the alien soak in sorrow, his face finally brightened as he thought of his friend Ruku. "My only friend Ruku!"

Raymond looked at his brother, before the two looked at their father and smiled. Edmond noticed the stare and knew what it meant; therefore, he quickly drove himself into the bathroom and closed the door.

"Whatever your idea is, no," Edmond yelled!

"Dad, tell mom we love her, but we have to make an interstellar phone call," Draymond shouted!

Azka turned his head from the television for the first time without sleeping and looked in the twin's direction. Whatever Draymond mentioned sounded hopeful and was frankly the only logical plan they had devised since they conned the Canadian Forces officers. Edmond thought his sons' idea was brilliant, therefore he got off the phone and helped them to reformat the device. They all moved into the garage where Draymond activated Max-X, while Raymond got the Orb and connected them together.

"Max-X, find a satellite that can connect an intergalactic phone call, then secure a safe line," Raymond instructed!

A few seconds later the 1963 Classic's onboard system responded, "A phoneline to the furthest reach of the universe, connected!"

"Orb, locate and connect phoneline with Ruku's spaceship," Draymond instructed!

"Command received, Draymond," replied the Orb!

The thought of once again hearing his friend's voice sent chills through the alien, who pulled closer to the vehicle. The computer system made a weird beeping sound as if it was dialling a number and continued doing so for nearly six minutes. Following the excitement of hearing his friend's voice, Azka's expectation simmered when he realized they may not acquire the connection. As the alien began turning away to return before the television, the beeping sound stopped and Ruku could be heard saying, "Orb, repair malfunction! Orb, repair malfunction!"

"Ruku, Ruku," Azka shouted!

"Azka! Is that you," Ruku exclaimed?

"Yes, my friend! Did your Orb detect foreign tracking signal sometime ago," Azka asked?

"Yes, I programed the coordinates, but I was unsure," Ruku stated!

"Use it to reach Planet Earth and hurry my friend," Azka begged?

On the fiftieth day of the siege, members from the Kingdom of Denmark had a private meeting with several other members of the United Nations Security Council, who believed they should forcefully retake their territory. During the meeting, Russian Federation members and China's Communist representatives argued that mankind is illustrating weakness by refusing to stand up to the aliens. Both nations contended that we must teach the aliens a lesson, for them to rethink their efforts to capture habited lands in the future. The leaders of Denmark were rather desperate to reclaim their territory and free their people being held hostage. Following such strong arguments, Denmark's officials decided to give the Zuruevians one final warning, before they blasted their spaceships from the sky.

At midday on the fifty-fifth day of the siege, Denmark provided their strongest reproach of the aliens, which came with a specific hour to strike. The Kingdom of Denmark's spokesperson fiercely stated in his message, "Confederation of Zurue, this will be your final warning! If your spaceships are not removed from Greenland's territory by twelve noon tomorrow, we will destroy your fleet!"

Following their multiple threats, news of Denmark's secret meeting was disclosed, therefore residents around the world feared what was to come. The great unknown caused tension across the planet, where people watch their clocks as if the world was scheduled to end. That night the Thornton men and their alien friend turned off the television and decided to play some fun games. The boys had been teaching Azka all they could about Earthlings and their ways of life, in hopes that both societies would peacefully end the conflict and coexist as neighbours. From all the games the twins taught Azka, his favorite became Charades, because he loved watching others do improvisation. They played until late into the night, where they all passed out and slept until 11am.

Once Edmond awakened the first thing he did was turn on the television, which was already on the news channel. The newscast producers placed a clock to the side of the news table that showed each second ticking down to midday. There was a different feel to the morning than usual, which led everyone to believe that the strikes were eminent. At 11:40am the long-range cannons aboard the Chinese and the Russian war ships began elevating and took aim at the circling spaceships. Watching the long-range cannons prepare to fire illustrated how serious the matter had gotten; therefore, Raymond, Azka, Edmond, and Draymond tightly held hands.

Everyone on the face of Mother Earth knew how significant such a strike would be, therefore even the servicemen on the warships felt conflicted about discharging their weapons. The skies were infested with numerous fighter jets from the different countries, that were launched to help protect the ships, should the aliens decide to attack. As fast as their jets were, watching the exploration vessels circled Greenland at the rate they did, sent fears through every pilot. The accuracy of the alien's Spec of Light was also rumoured, therefore the pilots were concerned about the alien technology they would be engaging.

At 11:58am the technicians aboard the International Space Station reported the arrival of seven humongous spaceships. News of the ships' arrival was quickly shared to International Intelligence Agencies across the globe. Despite the report, the aircraft carriers and warships that had their weapons aimed at the exploration vessels remained prepared to discharge. By the time word of the alien's motherships arrival reached news stations, there were only seconds left on the clock, before the cannons fired. Ten seconds before the canons' discharged, a humongous spaceship descended just below the clouds and held its position. With three seconds left on the clock, the six exploration vessels ascended to space behind the spaceship and left Greenland.

Azka and the Thornton males cheerfully shouted, before the youngsters and their alien friend started jumping around. As they pranced about the telephone rang with a weird ringtone unlike any they had ever heard. When Edmond picked up the phone and looked at the caller, the device highlighted several X's across the screen. The only calls they made from the phone were to Dee, Ruku, and Edmond's Uncle Alvin who owned the house, therefore, they felt nervous about answering.

"Hello," Edmond softly answered over the speaker!

"Azka, landing Explorer 29 at your location," Ruku exclaimed in Zuruevian.

Azka immediately began moving to the entrance, so everyone else followed him outside where Ruku was landing his exploration vessel on the front lawn of the property. The force of the engine expelled a lot of hot air, which blew dust all over. Once Ruku landed and turned off the engine, Azka rushed to the cockpit and lifted his friend from the vessel. Ruku could hardly stand or walk, so Azka hugged him gingerly before he led him over to introduce him to his new friends.

"Ruku these my friends Edmond, Draymond, and Raymond," Azka gladly introduced!

Their smiles immediately disappeared, when a team of Special Operative soldiers began jumping from bushes and hidden areas around the house. The team was led by Major Dilo and consisted of six armed soldiers, which included Second Lieutenant Crayguard and Sergeant Reacher. None of the soldiers were very happy about their detainees escaping or Earth's invasion, therefore, they were all in a foul mood.

"Nobody move," Major Dilo shouted! "If anybody so much as flinches, you will get shot!"

Edmond, Raymond, Draymond, and Azka slowly lifted their hands above their heads, but Ruku was a bit reluctant to do so. Following his incarceration, Azka knew how cruel the soldiers could be, so he advised his friend to do as the Earthlings ordered.

"Major Dilo, you can't detain Azka right now! You must allow him to fly to that mothership, to clarify what happened when he arrived here, or we will have an intergalactic war on our hands," Edmond begged?

"The only place you are all going to is a jail cell! As for this piece of space junk," Major Dilo threatened before he proceeded to open fire with his weapon at the exploration vessel!

"No," Azka yelled when he saw the damage done to the spacecraft!

"Harris, Mathews, cuff them," Major Dilo instructed two of his soldiers who lowered their rifles and removed handcuffs from their pouches to confine their detainees!

"Right back to where you belong, in jail," Second Lieutenant Crayguard told Edmond!

"I can't believe you soldiers want a war for millions of people to die! Your families," Raymond argued!

As the soldiers drew closer to the detained group to apply their restraints, Sergeant Reacher repositioned his rifle and aimed it at Major Dilo. The sergeant then grabbed the major and pulled him aside, while the others became unsure how to proceed.

"Change of plans boys, drop them! Raymond, Draymond, take their weapons," Sergeant Reacher stated!

"What are you doing Sergeant Reacher? You will go to jail for this," Major Dilo exclaimed!

The twins collected the soldiers' weapons and used their handcuffs to secure their hands. Major Dilo and his team were taken inside the house, where it would be much easier to control them.

"Sergeant Reacher, I thank you for truly listening to what we were saying," Edmond declared!

"Sorry that I didn't act sooner; that spaceship would still be operational," Sergeant Reacher responded!

"What are we going to do? Come on think," Draymond said!

"All is lost," Ruku warned!

"All is never lost with these Earthlings," Azka remarked!

"Why can't he just drive Grandpa's car," Raymond suggested?

"We don't have enough fuel for the trip. But maybe if we use the fuel from his explorer," Edmond said?

"I told you, all is never lost with these Earthlings," Azka lamented!

Azka began putting on his spacesuit while Edmond and Logan returned into the garage, where they made Max-X configured how to install the alien fuel. Draymond and Raymond were eager to inspect an explorer vessel, so they accompanied Ruku outside to detach the fuel cell. The alien ship was designed for the pilot to remove the container that held the fuel cell, which could be used to power almost anything. Ruku's Orb advised him how to remove the fuel cell, hence he retrieved the device and brought it into the garage.

It took Edmond and Logan several minutes to install the fuel cell, which had to be properly secured. When they finish the installation and turned the key inside the ignition, the 1963 Classic's engine turned over with a fierce roar. The twins were excited that the fuel experiment worked, yet they were saddened that they might never see Azka again. There was very little time to waste, and no guarantees Azka would reach his destination, therefore he issued his goodbyes to his friends and climbed into the car with Ruku. The Thornton males and Sergeant Reacher watched the vehicle fly off to outer space with the hopes of mankind aboard, knowing that should they fail, an interstellar war was guaranteed.

The unexpected arrival of their main convoy disrupted the treacherous actions of Junior Commandant Zonk and his marauders, who were seconds from achieving their objective. The Elite Academy's explorers were expected to ignite Earth's first intergalactic war, then maintained their assault until the main convoy arrived. Upon arrival into Earth's orbit, the Zuruevians began surveying the planet and observed the ongoing standoff over Greenland, therefore they dispatched a spaceship to intervene. Emperor Zura and his council members wanted answers for their many questions, therefore they ordered every returning vessel to the main ship. When Junior Commandant Zonk and the five Elite Academy flyers landed their exploration vessels on Emperor Zura's ship, everyone inside the station bowed their heads as their cockpit doors opened. Six pairs of female healers brought specially built carriages and transported the explorers to a recuperation station, where they pampered them while they properly regained their strengths.

Emperor Zura, his new pair of bodyguards, and seven of his counselors walked into the recuperation station, where all six explorers were recovering. Junior Commandant Zonk was already receiving praises for discovering Planet Earth, although there was no evidence that he did. The other five explorers had attested that Zonk was the first explorer here when they arrived, therefore he should be awarded the prize. For clarification on everything that happened, Zonk, was brought into a private meeting with the emperor and his delegates. The junior commander behaved as though he had undergone some form of psychosis, whereby he refrained from looking at anyone and spoke indecisively.

"Planet Zurue commends you for your discovery! But we must have your report," Emperor Zura said?

"Emperor Zura, I found this planet! Explorer 30 was here. When I detect his ship, I went to find him, and watched the Earthlings destroyed, Explorer 30," Junior Commandant Zonk explained!

"Does this mean we are now at war with the Earthlings," Council Member Four asked?

"Why did the Earthlings destroy Explorer 30," Council Member Nine shouted?

Emperor Zura raised his left hand, which stopped all the chatter. "What has transpired since?"

"I returned outer space and was confused, why Earthlings destroy Explorer 30!? While I study more about these Earthlings, my fellow explorers arrived. We could not allow the memory of Explorer 30 to go unchallenged, so we capture our new home, this, Greenland," Zonk exclaimed!

"I side with our Junior Commandant Zonk! If these Earthlings are barbarians, then we take our home by force," Lord Ozar exclaimed!

"I side with our Junior Commandant Zonk," Council Member 7 shouted!

"I also side with our Junior Commandant Zonk," Council Member 8 declared!

"I also support our Junior Commandant Zonk," Council Member 10 stated!

"I too support our Junior Commandant Zonk! Prepare the celebration festivities for his anointment, before we descend to this Earth and claim our new home," Emperor Zura stated prior to taking his exit!

Lord Ozar was the last councillor to leave the room and left a wrapped present on a side table. Junior Commandant Zonk picked up the present and slipped it beneath his robe, just before the healer returned to transport him back to the recuperation station. Emperor Zura's approval gave way to the preparations for Zonk's winning celebrations, therefore the events organizers began preparing for the festivities. While word went out about Zonk's celebration, news was delivered to Azka's family about his demise at the hands of the Earthlings.

Within three Earth hours the festivities were prepared, and all the important dignitaries were transferred onto the emperor's ship. Junior Commandant Zonk and his five astronaut's family members were brought to the event to help celebrate their achievements. Although the Elite Academy flyers failed at their mission, their primary objective was still achievable. The nations of Earth had publicly declared their first major warning, which threatened the aliens against any travel onto the planet. As long as both parties refrained from any discussions, the Elite explorers and Lord Ozar's objectives were achieved.

There was so much joy among the Zuruevians that the interior stadium in which they held their celebrations, was packed with thousands of party enthusiasts who were all excited to thank Zonk for his discovery. The celebrations were also being broadcasted on large screens on the other spaceships for all who could not attend. Regardless of what was to come, the Zuruevians had been in space for years and were only thrilled that they found a habitable planet. Junior Commandant Zonk's five comrades were brought out and honoured, before the grand winner was presented, in all his glory. Zuruevians cheered and shouted Zonk's name throughout the stadium, as he made his way to the podium to collect his prize.

Azka trusted the Thorntons and felt comfortable travelling to space in their street vehicle, but his friend Ruku began questioning their safety from the moment they left the garage. As the 1963 Classic approached Earth's Ozone Layer, Ruku became increasingly nervous and began asking, "If the car was equipped to shield them from the heat?" After they successfully passed through, Ruku's confidence level raised slightly, although he would have preferred remaining on Earth.

With Emperor Zura's handlers throughout the ship all in attendance at the stadium, his navigation crew left the controls on autopilot until their return. When the spaceship detected the flying object, the onboard computing system categorized the car as a threat and initiated its defensive protocol. As the targeting device prepared to discharge, both Azka and Ruku's Orbs reconnected to the system and deactivated the defense response. The Orbs also opened the aviation hangar door, which enabled the 63 Classic to fly aboard.

It took Azka sometime; however, he had managed to figure out what the Elite Academy's secret mission code-named, 'Anarchy' was expected to achieve. Those who were behind the plot did not wish to negotiate or accept a piece of any planet, but rather annihilate whatever species already existed for total dominance. Although there were no guarantees their military force would be sufficient to gain a victory, Lord Ozar and his followers disregarded everything else and chose war. Lord Ozar knew that with a war already ongoing once the general population arrived, Emperor Zura would be forced to engage and fight until there was a victor. Each scenario that Azka thought of required the death of their emperor for Zork's master to take control, therefore he realized their ultimate plot was to assassinate Emperor Zura.

According to Zuruevian law, Zonk, could be the only slayer of their emperor who their population would permit. To stop the Junior Commandant from completing his master's wishes, Azka had to reach the stadium before he got close enough to the emperor. Their only means of getting there fast was to borrow the twin's hoverboards, in the back of the car. Both he and Ruku leapt from the car and stepped onto the hovering skateboards, which were a foot off the floor. Ruku had never ridden a skateboard, so as soon as he went a few yards he fell off. Despite tumbling the ride seemed quite enjoyable, therefore he was determined to master it. When Ruku tried the second time he fell once more, but with each attempt he went further and further.

"Go, don't worry about me, I will catch up," Ruku told Azka!

Just before Azka reached the stadium's entrance, Ruku sped by him and cheered as he went by, to boast that he had mastered the hoverboard. Once Azka saw his friend easily handling the hoverboard, he quickly caught up and raced to the stadium. The cheers and shouting from inside the stadium could be heard well beyond the large, sealed doors. Neither Ruku nor Azka had ever boarded one of the evacuation spaceships, and were light-years away when they launched, so both explorers were extremely impressed with the designs.

The crowd inside the stadium went silent, and the explorers could hear Emperor Zura beginning to address them. "Zuruevians! The one responsible for finding our new home, Junior Commandant Zonk!"

As the crowd started to cheer even louder, Azka and Ruku rode onto the stadium grounds fully dressed in their spacesuits. Junior Commandant Zonk was making his way across the stage towards Emperor Zura and froze when he saw the two explorers. The crowd immediately went silent, as everybody watched with keen interest to see whose faces were inside the helmets. Neither of the two friends unveiled their identities and slowly hoverboarded across the grounds over to the stage. Zonk looked over at Lord Ozar with confusion; however, his master signalled him to kill the emperor. While walking onto the stage, Azka observed when Junior Comman-dant Zonk started rushing towards Emperor Zura and withdrew a rigid blade. To save his emperor, Azka threw the hoverboard at Zonk, who got knocked off his feet and fell on the stage. The emperor's guards quickly rush in and sedated Zonk before they carried him away. Emperor Zura picked up the knife and stared at it, before he looked over at his council members. Chief Commander Ibik, Second Commander Xong and Third Commander Kzaw were trying to sneak their way from the venue, but the guards took them into custody.

Azka walked onto the stage and removed his helmet beside his friend Ruku. Many of those in the crowd re-leased a huge sigh, after hearing that Azka had perished. Emperor Zura opened his arms and gave Azka and Ruku huge hugs, knowing he would have gotten killed had it not been for their efforts.

"Emperor Zura! I sent the tracking signal, you followed to get here! I, found Earth," Azka remarked!

The emperor needed no further confirmation and declared, "Azka, the discoverer of Earth!"

Everyone in attendasnce cheered loudly for Azka, especially his friend and colleague Ruku.

The Zuruevians continued partying and celebrated their newest hero. Ruku and Azka's family members were transferred onto the emperor's ship to reunite and celebrate with them. Contrary to the Elite flyers, the two friends were extremely happy to see their family members and spent quality time together alone. Emperor Zura and his fifteen council members gathered the next day inside their meeting hall to discuss how they should contend with the Earthlings. Azka and Ruku were invited by the emperor, who had chosen to have them join his cabinet as ministers.

"Emperor Zura, what are we to do about the Earthlings," Council Member 11 asked?

"They have declared war if we enter their planet," Council Member 7 stated!

"We have nowhere else to turn! It could take centuries for us to find another home," Council Member 6 added!

"You have been misled about the Earthlings! We can find a home here without war," Azka said.

"And how are we to do that," Council Member 10 asked?

"We talk with them and explain our ordeal. We can keep looking for another planet, while we rest here, temporarily," Ruku suggested!

"I believe it is too early for us to live among that many Earthlings, on this Greenland," Council Member 8 argued!

"Then we negotiate for a piece of Antarctica! There is more land there and less people," Azka responded.

"But what will these Earthlings want in return," Council Member 2 enquired?

"With our energy source, it will not cost much," Azka declared.

"Then who do we negotiate with," Council Member 4 asked?

"I know the perfect Earthling," Azka stated!

Following Azka and Ruku's departure to try and stop the escalating tensions between their species and mankind, Edmond and Logan released their captives. Major Dilo and his soldiers immediately took the four traitors into custody then transferred them back to base. Edmond, Draymond, Raymond, and Logan were placed inside the same detainment facility they held Azka. When they arrived and Colonel Dibbs heard what happened, the military commander threatened to charge them with espionage and every other applicable charge there was. There were all sorts of activities ongoing around the base, which involved soldiers transferring weapons from one area to the next as well as others repositioning artillery to aim upwards.

Every major country around the world began preparing their military for war. While members of the armed forces prepared for an alien invasion, peace activists around the world took to the streets in drones to protest their government's response to the situation. News exerts had begun spreading about the destruction of Planet Zurue, therefore, many opposers began siding with the aliens. Contrary to the governments' hostile response, high tech giants wanted to convey a different message and thus extended an invitation over their satellites for the aliens to come to the negotiations table.

Several hours after their initial detainment, Colonel Dibbs personal opened the confinement door and politely asked the detainees to step out. Edmond had received a new position as the first alien negotiator on Earth, while Logan got promoted to being a general. With such an important job description, Edmond went from a detainment holding to having his personal security detail, who ensured that he remained safe. All four males went from being considered traitors to being celebrated as heroes for their bravery.

Five days later the largest spectacle in Earth's history occurred, when Emperor Zura, four of his council members, and two of his guards arrived at the United Nations Security Building in New York. Following their impressive entrance, wherein they landed their spaceship just outside the entrance, dignitaries from across the globe lined the walkway to be introduced. Once inside the meeting hall, Edmond addressed the nations of leaders on behalf of the Zuruevians and negotiated a piece of legislation and land ownership for Earthling's newest neighbours.

Azka drove the 1963 Classic back to the Thornton's family home with Ruku following in a two-passenger spaceship. As he landed the vehicle on the front driveway, Draymond, Raymond, and Edmond came out to greet him. The radio inside the car was on and Azka was listening to a female reporter delivering the day's newscast. "For the first time in our history we have neighbours living here who are not humans! Yes, ladies and gentlemen, we have officially welcomed the Zuruevians from Planet Zurue here on Planet Earth; and humans worldwide are quite taken by the idea! Mind you, they love living in those cold climates, which is why they down there in Antarctica, but from me to the Zuruevians, on behalf of Earthlings, welcome to Planet Earth baby!"

Draymond and Raymond greeted their friend as soon as he stepped from the vehicle, while Ruku landed the double passenger spaceship off to the side, then came over to greet their friends.

"Thanks Azka, for making me the primary negotiator between the Zuruevians and Earth's governments. That is what got the Canadian Government to drop those charges against us! I'm heading down to Antarctica in two days to come see Emperor Zura, if you want, I'll carry the boys along for you guys to catch up," Edmond offered before he fist-bumped both aliens and went inside?

"I look forward to their visit," Azka stated!

"So how are you guys liking Antarctica," Raymond asked?

"Amazing! Never been anywhere like it, the animals, the birds, the fishes," Azka said!

"I saw you and your emperor at the United Nations the other day," Draymond remarked!

"Yes, there is so many meetings and negotiations with different countries! I am off to another meeting after I leave here," Azka said!

"That's awesome, my best Zuruevian friend is a dignitary," Raymond answered!

"I look forward to seeing you twins when you come to Antarctica! But business calls," Azka answered before he fist bumped the twins and left with Ruku!

"See you soon," Draymond exclaimed as they waived goodbye!

The End

www.ingramcontent.com/pod-product-compliance
Lightning Source LLC
Chambersburg PA
CBHW041431300726
48981CB00008B/430